Nur Elme~~~~~~~~~~~~~~~~~~~~rew
up there a~~~~~~~~~~~~~~~ned a BA and MA in
English and Comparative Literature from the
American University in Cairo. In 1991 she obtained a
PhD at Cambridge University for her research on T.S.
Eliot. She is now living in Cairo, teaching at the
American University and working for *Al-Ahram
Weekly*. She is co-editor and co-translator with Eva
Elias of *In the Cold Night: A Bilingual Edition of
Stories by Muhamed El-Makhzingi*, Cairo 1993.

Abdelwahab Elmessiri was born in Egypt in 1938. He
studied at Alexandria University and went on to the
US to obtain his MA and PhD in English and
Comparative Literature. He has taught English
Literature at universities in Egypt, Saudi Arabia and
Kuwait. He is at present Professor Emeritus at Ain
Shams University in Egypt. Many of his writings have
been published in Arabic and English, and he has con-
tributed to numerous periodicals and journals on a
wide range of subjects.

A Land of Stone and Thyme

An Anthology of Palestinian Short Stories

edited by Nur and Abdelwahab Elmessiri

QUARTET BOOKS

To all mothers who live to remember their children –
Palestinian or otherwise

First published by Quartet Books Limited 1996
A member of the Namara Group
27 Goodge Street
London W1P 2LD

Translation copyright © by Nur and Abdelwahab Elmessiri 1996

ISBN 0 7043 7092 1

A catalogue record for this book is available from the British Library

Printed and bound in Great Britain by BPC Paperbacks Ltd.

Contents

Introduction

1 A Brief History of the Palestinian Short Story

It could be argued that the 1920s witnessed the birth of the Palestinian short story. The first generation of short-story writers, among whom Khalil Baidus was the most prominent, learned narrative techniques through translation, adapatation and imitation of models drawn mostly from Europe. Their literary output was of little artistic value, largely because of their strong didactic tendencies.

When a second generation emerged in the 1930s, the most eminent of its members was Mahmoud Seifeddin al-Irani. His stories had a pronounced socialist bias and were strongly influenced by the Russian writer Maxim Gorky. This is clearly evident in his first collection *Awwalu al-shawt (The Start of the Course)* published in 1937, and in his second *Maa al-naas (With the People)*. His works, though courageous attempts to portray the desperate social reality of the Palestinian people, were lacking in subtlety and ambiguity. Intellectual and social issues were too clearly defined, characters remained largely flat and the tone was sentimental. His later stories, however, show intellectual and artistic maturity. The one-dimensional characters give way to more rounded ones who interact with their surroundings and respond to events in a more complex manner. Many writers, among them Nagati Sidki, Issa al-Bunduk, Yohana Descartes, Abdallah Mukhlis and Mohamed Darwaza, followed al-Irani's lead. This trend developed throughout the 1940s, acquiring more subtlety in the works of Aref al-Azouni, Emile Habibi, Najwa Qawar and Asma Touba. Besides these social realists, there were other writers who directed their attention to self-exploration, for example Abdulamid Yasin with his collection *Aqaasiis (Tales)* published in 1946. Also to be noted are some of the early stories of Jabra Ibrahim Jabra and the works of Mohamed Adib al-Ameri. The whole spectrum of Palestinian stories of the time expressed the involvement of most Palestinians with their national cause and struggle. Excessive national zeal and sentimentality tended at times to undermine technical considerations, and the tone of many stories was often too shrill and explicit.

There was a radical change after 1948, due to the disruption and dislocation that Palestinian society experienced. A new situation had arisen and therefore new themes were dealt with and an almost entirely new sensibility developed. Post-1948 stories expressed the frustrations of the people, their nostalgia for their lost homeland and their dream of returning to it. The Palestinians found themselves flung headlong into the day-to-day world of Arab politics and the Palestinian national struggle became inextricably linked with the nationalist ideology of Arab political parties and movements. Some stories, drawing upon new resources, depicted the acts of heroism and sacrifice that sprang from a deep attachment to the land and brooded over the events and forces that had led to the disaster. The hopelessness, desperation and sadness of the refugees' situation became a central theme of many short stories. A curious combination of a highly sentimental tone and an undue concern with the political pervaded the stories of the 1950s. This proved to be confining since it restricted the writers to the merely political dimension of reality or to a morbid and at times maudlin obsession with national woes. Some stories were largely cries of pain or mouthpieces for revolutionary slogans, populated with heroes who believed in the noblest of ideals and the highest of principles.

That does not mean, however, that we cannot find well-structured, more artistically sophisticated stories. We can refer to Samira Azzam's collection of stories, *Al-Zillu al-Kabir* (*The Big Shadow*) as well as to the stories of Jabra Ibrahim Jabra and Ghassan Kanafani. The latter made an enormous contribution to the laying down of the artistic and social idiom of the Palestinian short story.

In the 1960s a new generation of writers appeared both inside and outside Palestine. Apart from those by Habibi, Azzam and Kanafani, all the stories in this anthology are from the output of this generation. Some of these writers – Mahmoud Shuqair, Yehia Yakhlaf, Rashad Abu Shawer and Ahmed Omar Shaheen – lived outside occupied Palestine. This diaspora gave their stories a specificity rooted in the diversity of their surroundings and experiences. The themes of the Wandering Palestinian and of life in the camps figure prominently in their stories.

On the other hand, writers living inside occupied Palestine had to contend with an oppressive occupying authority which literally restricted the movement of writers and hounded any whose works manifested a hint of political involvement. To overcome this severe handicap, some simply confined themselves to their own narrow inner universe. Others, like Emile Habibi, Mohamed Ali Taha, Mohamed Naffaa and Zaki Darwish, resorted to symbolism and allusion.

The style of this generation was influenced to a considerable extent by a large body of world literature which had become available for the first time in translation. Serious critical review and evaluation, moreover, had evolved, thereby helping writers to develop critical insight into their own works and hence become more disciplined. As a result, writers began to explore more complex dimensions of human existence and to free themselves from the stranglehold that events had previously had on their imagination. The Palestinian short story had finally matured, leaving behind its emotional, intellectual and artistic adolescence. These innovators gave free range to their imagination, employing a variety of expressive and narrative techniques to tell anew the story of their society and their oppressed people, both under occupation and in the diaspora.

2 Literary Introduction to the Stories in this Anthology

The story of the stories

Read as a unified whole, in order of appearance, the short stories of this anthology combine to form a myth and are each a facet of a meta-narrative or framework which has been imposed upon them. The stories have been grouped into six sections: Shadows of Paradise Lost; Exile from the Land; Refugees in Hostile Cities; Babel; Death-in-Life/ Life-in-Death; and Dreams of Paradise Redeemed. These, read in sequence, tell a single story. A child, or two children or a group of friends, at any rate a naïve protagonist, plays near a tree when suddenly the game or the place of play becomes soured: paradise is lost. The playground becomes the land from which the protagonist is dispossessed and he or she finds himself or herself in exile, amid alien corn, still dreaming of that which has been lost. The protagonist is subjected to further trials

4

and tribulations as a refugee in a hostile city into which he or she tries half-heartedly to assimilate: the diaspora, after all, whether eternal or not, must be endured. The alien city, unlike the alien countryside, is so far removed from what has been lost that our protagonist fails abysmally to communicate with the inhabitants of this strange place: half-hearted attempts at assimilation are not possible in Babel. Where language fails in Babel, with it fails memory and a state of death-in-life engulfs the protagonist – though at this moment and in this place of utter loss, this underworld, there are flickerings of renewal, of life-in-death. Finally, the protagonist returns to the site of play – not quite the same tree, not quite the same game – and recognizes, though does not necessarily come to repossess, that which has been lost.

'Wait for me by the ancient *gemeiz* tree near the border of our land,' begins Ahmed Omar Shaheen's story 'The Tree', which opens the first section of the anthology, **Shadows of Paradise Lost**. Mere waiting by the tree which used to be 'like a mother', however, is no longer possible because one day 'it happened': 'the bandits joined forces' and 'together they tied a strong rope around the thick trunk of the tree and with red hot irons they branded it'. Thus possessed, 'the tree was no longer the tree [that the two childhood friends] remembered', and one of them leaves to go about 'his task' while the other remains at a loss regarding the place of waiting. Just as the 'honey-sweet' fruits of Shaheen's tree turn sour with insects and rats boring into them, the game called Boys and Girls in Mohamed Ali Taha's story 'A Boy and Girl from Deheisha' turns into a new game called Soldiers and Patriots. The children wanted to play a game but Thabit, the boy from Deheisha, 'made it for real'. He made them play a game which Samiha, the girl from Deheisha who loves Thabit, finds 'sad and desolate'. Samiha longs for a house, one very similar to that which Hassan and Zeinab draw with their crayons in Rashad Abu Shawer's story 'A Green House

5

with a Brick-Red Roof'. Like them, she makes a drawing with 'a radiant sun', like them, she comes to her end suddenly, and, like them, her drawing lives beyond her: Samiha's sun becomes a 'yellow orange' falling into the vase upon which her mother ponders. At the foot of the drawing of a green and red house, orange trees and a bird which the children had painted, the inscription 'Hassan loves Zeinab' has the last word in Abu Shawer's story. In Farouk Wadi's 'The Bird', which ends the **Shadows of Paradise Lost** section, however, 'the flock of night crows' have the last word. 'They circle above' the heads of the villagers who had been visited by love, a colourful bird, 'one smiley-sun day', and draw 'terrible shapes'.

The maternal tree becomes a 'decrepit octopus', amusing games turn into torture sessions, a drawing of a dream house is incinerated in an explosion, a colourful bird is replaced by 'pitch-black crows'. Paradise itself, as are even mere shadows or dreams thereof, is lost.

The hearth, however, in exile is perhaps all the more real for that, and innocence less vulnerable. At a family gathering, the blind Sheikh Issa of Rasmi Abu Ali's story 'Kurza' is adamant that, should the others elders listen to him and end their exile, not by returning home but by going to Kurza, they will they find 'a garden, a paradise beneath which rivers flow'. He is humoured for that evening – 'no one dared remind [this avuncular figure] he was blind' – and just for that one night everyone sleeps happily dreaming of 'the promised paradise, Kurza'. In 'Stealing Away, We Returned', also by Abu Ali, the young narrator and his mother do return to al-Malha, the village from which they had been deported, 'like thieves in the night' to steal their own clothes and, in the case of the little boy, to collect what his mother finds to be useless junk: a broken serving spoon and some schoolbooks, among which is a Qur'an. There they find other al-Malha women, also 'stealing' – in their case, the unpicked olive harvest – each careful not to 'trespass on another's patch, but [gathering] only from her own. This, in spite of the fact that they had been dispossessed of the land and all that was on it.' The strength of 'the force of habit and the sense of property' are also visible in Akram Shareem's story 'The Land'. After being moved out at gunpoint from their village on the West Bank of Jordan, the people of Qalqiliya return. 'Every family sat in the place where its house had been, and they became neighbours once again . . . Each family set up its tent poles where its old house had been.' In Mohamed Naffaa's story 'Kushan Number 4: Because We Love the Land', when a neighbour asks the thirteen-year-old narrator's father '"Why are you going to the field? The field is gone,"' he answers, thereby bringing the story and the second section of the anthology to a close, 'clearly and with confidence, "Because we love the land."' Domesticity and wheat harvesting, so we are momentarily led to believe, will continue unbroken.

But not for long. Our narrators in Section III of this anthology, **Refugees in Hostile Cities**, have aged, fallen in love, become separated from their loved ones and are now refugees, not in a nearby village or little town which they can think of as 'the same place' (as does the narrator of 'Stealing Away, We Returned'), let alone in their own demolished village, but in cities like Amman, Beirut, Kuwait, Tunis, Cairo and in refugee camps. The problems become more complex, the narrators more bewildered, the forces of hostility and enmity less localized and the cosy domesticity of the family no longer a possibility. True, there are moments of bewilderment and panic in the previous section, **Exile from the Land**, but there the characters are in a confrontational position *vis-à-vis* the cause of such bewilderment. And because the forces pushing them into exile are but a stone's throw away, the narrators of the previous section are more centred and, as subjects, less dispersed.

The protagonist in Section III 'roams the streets and the alleys of the city' as the father separated from his wife and

children in Salih Abu Isbaa's 'Dead is the Yearning'.
Separated from his pregnant wife, Mariam, who died in an
attack on the camp, he might, as in Rashad Abu Shawer's
'Pizza in Memory of Mariam', order a pizza and de-
liberately proceed to get drunk, having failed to liberate
Palestine and himself, a Palestinian. In this section of the
anthology, more than in any other, the protagonist is a
'Palestinian' in spite of attempts at being naturalized in
and assimilated into alien cities. 'By this title [the
Palestinian] they called and knew him [the protagonist of
Samira Azzam's story] and cursed him if the need arose.
Just like the Armenian cobbler he had known in his
boyhood, who had spent thirty years of his wretched life
mending and patching shoes for a neighbourhood where
nobody bothered, let alone needed, to find out if his name
was Hagop . . . or Sarkis or Vartan.' As the protagonist of
Azzam's story knows too well, a Palestinian lacks the
documents (ID, passport, travel document) necessary to
be able to cross, unharassed and uninterrogated, 'the
crooked black lines on the maps'. Instead, he or she will be
betrayed by his or her accent, as is the protagonist of
Badr's 'The Trellised Vine' or, worse still, will be forced to
leave, perhaps at gunpoint, for 'a country called Lebanon',
as is the protagonist of Mahmoud Shuqair's story 'The
Homeland'. This is, after all, exile, an exile less immediately felt, but all the more engulfing and encompassing
for that, than the one of the previous section of the
anthology. It is, as the protagonist of Badr's 'The Trellised
Vine' reflects, the 'era of the North. The North of Africa,
the North of Lebanon, the North of anywhere, or the left
of it – Lebanon or elsewhere.'

Separated from his or her family in this era of the North,
the protagonist is subjected to continual interrogation
and confinement, whether in the sense of claustrophobia
or literally in prison. In Wadi's 'Black Lines', 'the faces of
relatives and friends fixed their questioning glances' on
the protagonist who is 'without a city and without a

woman', continually asking, 'Did you find work?' The Palestinian is interrogated by the Jordanian authorities about his ID papers. Doctors, waiter and friends keep asking the protagonist of 'Pizza in Memory of Mariam' why he drinks so much. He receives no answer as to why Mariam and their unborn child died, just as in Abu Isbaa's story the elderly man who chooses to ignore the difference between Ramallah (the town from which he has been exiled and to which he returns illegally) and al-Ramla (the town to which he has been exiled and in which he lives alone) finds no answer to the question, 'How could we have parted . . . And now, where are they?' Summoned for interrogation, he too is 'asked question after question', the same question – '"What brought you from al-Ramlah to Ramallah?"' Even the bourgeois narrator of 'The Trellised Vine' who, after finishing her workout session at the nearby gymnasium, decides to pick a few leaves from a vine, is not safe from a flurry of questions which, though lighthearted, are not without the edge of, '"You're Palestinian."' Nor do mythical figures like Joha, in Mohamed Ali Taha's story, whose profession is '"to sow smiles on people's faces"' and whose address is '"around the stoves in homes"', escape being led into a dark room by a jailor.

'"What are you doing here?"' – the same question to which Badr's aerobics-outfitted protagonist and that of Abu Isbaa's story are subjected – opens Shuqair's story 'The Homeland' and is followed by the protagonist's imprisonment. The same question is echoed in the closing section of the story, which, in turn, closes Section III of the anthology. But this time, instead of a hostile soldier, it is a *fedai* who asks the question. '"What did you do?"' after '"the strange wind [blew] over [your] homeland"' until '"it was lost?"' the *fedai* asks the protagonist, not reproachfully as the parents' faces in Wadi's 'Black Lines', nor threateningly, as the soldier asks, 'What are you doing here?' in the opening of the story. The protagonist of 'The

Homeland' – like the pregnant Yusra of Badr's 'A Land of Stone and Thyme', the story which opens this section, who is kept awake by dreams of her husband's missing photo and who ruefully remarks, 'What am I do then? Wait? Life has been nothing but waiting upon waiting...' – 'has come to hate waiting' and is '[kept] from sleeping' by his 'mother's voice'. He follows the *fedai*. (*Fedaiyin* figure as strongly as the 'Palestinian' in this section.) No longer an aimless wanderer, half-heartedly seeking a return to the homeland through reminiscences of fairytales or the pursuit of women's bodies, the protagonist of 'The Homeland' 'walked behind [the young *fedai*] from road to road, becoming more confident the further down the road [he] ventured. The bullets were pouring down like rain...'

And nature in this section of the anthology is indeed a hostile force, almost colluding, as the narrator of 'Stealing Away, We Returned' remarks, with the catastrophe that befell an entire people. The rain, the sea and the wind are all either frustratingly mute as in 'The Homeland' or positively terrifying as in 'Pizza in Memory of Mariam'. The mother in Badr's 'A Land of Stone and Thyme' 'would stay up all night, too frightened to sleep. The wind would beat against the plastic sheets and would bang against the transparent oilcloths [used as makeshift window panes] making sounds like the bombing.' But though 'the bullets were pouring down like rain' in Shuqair's 'The Homeland', 'the young man's rifle shook, towering in space'.

Whereas the stories in Section III are set in specific cities or towns, in Section IV, **Babel**, the setting is vague. Bewilderment borders on madness and confused yearnings and dreams become nightmares. Crooked lines drawn on maps by others become spiders spinning their webs inside the protagonist's head, as in Ghassan Kanafani's 'Nothing'. Interrogation and semblances of conversation persist but – and this is the point of this section – they are pointless. The disappearance of lines determining place, crooked though those lines might be –

that is to say, the despecification of space or the loss of place – is parallel in this section to a loss of the possibility of shared meaning. The sharing of meaning presupposes a desire to leave one's specific ground for a common one; the commonplace is attendant upon a negotiation of differences, a crossing of boundaries. But difference and not indifference is the starting point. Most of the stories in **Babel** tell, as in Zaki Darwish's story, of 'how boundaries totally disappeared, how things became confused and how the search for truth became an imaginary subject'.

The 'nothing' which the Palestinian soldier who opened fire on the occupied territory gives in reply to the Israeli psychiatrist is the counterpart to the 'nothing' which the Israeli driver sees when driving through the countryside with a Palestinian passenger. A land without a people, thus a people without intentionality. Conversation, as in Jamal Naji's story 'A Conversation', leads nowhere, even when both parties are speaking in Arabic, and one in perfect, classical Arabic at that. It certainly leads nowhere when one of the concerned parties does 'not even bother to look' at the other. No meeting point is possible if, as in Kanafani's 'The Crucified Sheep', doctors in a caravan headed for Mecca tell a bedouin in need of water for his dying sheep that 'cars . . . need water'.

When conversation does lead somewhere it results, in the case of the narrator of 'A Conversation' which takes place in a moving bus, in his missing his stop, seeing 'through the windows his house receding into the distance', and to his '[forgetting] entirely [his] right to share the seat' with the interlocutor who did not deign to make room for him. Less bewildered is the narrator of Riyad Baidas's story 'Flying Carpet', which also takes place in a moving vehicle. He is amused by the suspicion with which he is viewed by the man who offers him a lift. '"Learning a language is one thing and what's going on inside my head is another"' is his reply to the driver's contention that '"had [he] learned Arabic, [he] would have been able to imagine what's going on inside [his passenger's] head."' On the other hand, the doctors in Kanafani's story 'Nothing' claim to know what is inside the Palestinian gunman's head, for they are the ones who define 'the term "nervous breakdown"', who determine it by asking 'special questions' and who determine the difference between a 'medical case' and a 'military case'. After a futile attempt at conversation with the nurse, the gunman patient finally gives in to the doctors' definition of his case, 'the inside of his forehead [becoming] as clear as a white marble slab'. Collusion, so it seems, is the only road to a common language. Conversation, unless willingly undertaken as such by both parties concerned, leads, so the narrator of 'A Conversation' learns, to forgetting about the whole point, namely, the desire to negotiate for a shared commonplace or ground.

But apart from 'Nothing', 'Flying Carpet' and 'The Conversation' – and in 'A Conversation' evidence of the antagonist's nationality is slim indeed, and, if anything, problematic – none of the stories in **Babel** sets up the question of non-communication within an explicitly Palestinian–Israeli framework. In fact, the rest of the stories – except for Mahmoud al-Rimawi's 'A Chapter from the Book of Present Days', a satire on media responses to political calamities which damns Arab, American, European and Israeli governments alike – are not even set within any explicit political context. Mohamed Tamila's 'Fear' and 'The City' are set in surrealistically empty cities. In the former, the narrator, who is going for a walk, begins by thinking that a running man telling him to 'run away' is mad and ends, after several similar encounters, with the narrator himself running and telling others to run away. In 'The City', strangely inhabited solely by old people, the narrator is thought of as mad for claiming and insisting to be in his thirties, and ends with the narrator falling to the floor upon seeing

12

himself, as the others had seen him we are meant to infer, in the mirror. Zaki Darwish's 'The Man Who Lies a Lot' probes the issue of deceit and self-deception, of the gap between the fictions of the narrator's designs, on the one hand, and the reality, not of his choosing, on the other. In Darwish's story, the father's ugly lie becomes a reality in spite of himself – his daughter does get eaten after all – while in Tamila's story 'The Shoes', the lie becomes an idea that the schoolgirl narrator rather likes. She had lied about her shoe size when a charity 'committee' came to her school, because she did not know what her size was, and wound up with shoes far too big for her. When questioned by a classmate about why she is not wearing her new shoes, she lies again and says that she will save them for a feast day. Very quickly, however, the lie becomes a plan embraced, a viable possibility. The babbling of unpremeditated shoe sizes to authority figures in command of a language to which children have no access – 'I didn't know that feet had sizes. But I'd once heard that one of our relatives had asked his brother who was going to Saudi Arabia to get him a pair of shoes, size 42, so I immediately said, "I am size 42"' – proves to be an admirable tactical move and the girl decides to 'come back for them when [she is] older'. Very different this babbling from the long-range planning of the father figure of Darwish's story.

The inevitability, even perhaps desirability, of Babel, and also the desirability of the attempt to transcend it – and transcend it only having gone through it, participated in it and listened to its noise – is perhaps best illustrated in Kanafani's story 'The Slope'. In this story, a teacher finds himself in the position of a student. In a school without textbooks, one way of filling class time is to allow a student to tell his classmates the story of his father the cobbler. The boy provides different endings to his story – in a world of competing listeners and inter-pretations, such relativity is perhaps necessary. In his own way, the boy accommodates Babel, knowing full well that, though principal and classmate each wants to hear a different ending, a sense of an ending and of closure is what they both want. In spite of this, he himself knows that his kaleidoscopic story, even if broken down into multiple interpretations, is unified by his own certainty that '[his] father doesn't die', that '[he] just said that so [he] could finish the story', and that 'if [he] hadn't, [the story] wouldn't ever have finished'.

From the certainty that one's father lives on, the historical need for endings notwithstanding, we move in Section V, **Death-in-Life/Life-in-Death**, to the almond blossom unremembered. In Emile Habibi's 'At Last the Almond Blossomed', the main character, Mister M, experiences, he knows not why, an overwhelming sense of joy at the sight of almond trees in blossom, and then gradually remembers the connection between the blossom and a beautiful love story of a schoolfriend. Mister M had 'truly forgotten that he himself is the hero of the beautiful love story', and the narrator, his friend, is left wondering if he could 'bring back the dead' and end Mister M's estrangement from this all but buried past. In Shaheen's 'A Summons', the narrator is put to the test by his grandmother to see if he is indeed her 'awaited relative', and though he recognizes her, she inexplicably turns to 'face the wall', claiming that 'a stranger' has been brought to trifle with her. Recognition, the linking of time past with time present, fails in these stories, each side of the stump is left to wither. Alienation of one generation from the next is also poignantly expressed in Kanafani's 'With Both of His Hands', a horrific story of an ageing father who, abandoned by his son, is driven four years later to conduct an experiment, the result of which is vampirism on the part of a starving male kitten, with an older male cat as its victim.

The most extreme state of abjection in this section of the anthology is that portrayed in Hassan Hemeid's story

'A Madman's Awakening', narrated from the point of view of the corpse of a madman who, awakened by two indifferent angels (who could have easily made an appearance as authority figures in **Babel**), wonders panic-stricken if the people of the camp have returned home, forgetting, in their haste to end their exile, to bid him farewell. To his dismay, he realizes, looking up helplessly through a hole in his grave, that the people of the camp are being deported and the camp itself is about to be bulldozed. The angels then compel him to go back 'to dwelling in [his] sleep. But [he] did not fall asleep.'

The last four stories of the section also more or less centre on a corpse, but these stories speak more of life-in-death, of order emerging out of chaos and decomposition, than of death-in-life. Shaheen's lyrical 'Four Colours' is told from the point of view of a *fedai* being shot, and then, perhaps, dying. The reader does not become fully aware of the fact that this is a swan-song till the closing sentence of the story. 'I rose with the water gushing sky high, like a butterfly bedewed with drizzle, embracing the tune, the flowers and the fragrance, and shrouded in a rainbow of four colours.' In the funeral procession in al-Rimawi's story, the narrator, a close friend of the deceased comrade, together with the other friends carrying the coffin, feels it shake and sees the head stir just before the dust pours down to bury it. Though dead, the mother in Shaheen's story 'The Earth', 'is still capable of giving birth to a creature who speaks, like Christ, in the crib'. She is very similar to Um al-Khayr in Tawfiq Fayyad's story who undoes the metamorphosis from beautiful Mother of Goodness to a body covered with festering sores (which had been wrought upon her by a snake) and is changed into an ancient gnarled tree which, as the child narrators 'grew older', 'grew bigger in the distance until its green branches contained all the houses in the village'. This in spite of the fact that all the villagers, with the exception of her lover, Hassan the ploughman, had shunned her, losing their faith in her after she had been bitten by the snake. 'Not even death could get the better of' [her]' just as the contraceptive pills that the dead mother in Shaheen's 'The Earth' was made to swallow could not prevent her from being fertile.

The paradise regained and the return in the final section of the anthology is not so much a reappropriation of land as it is a recovery of certainty regarding a redemptive dream. The tree of Abu Shawer's story, unlike that of Shaheen's which opened **Shadows of Paradise Lost**, does not die to the children who make the decision that its leaves would remain green, in spite of half of it being burnt by a missile. In Abu Shawer's 'The Tree', the birds, similar in spirit to Wadi's colourful bird in **Shadows of Paradise Lost**, are not, as in Wadi's bird, defeated by the crows (in this case, B52 warplanes), but rather, 'keep singing and singing until a leaf sprouts amidst the dead branches . . . then they fly away . . . to return the next day . . . and so on'. And though in Asqalani's 'Breaking the Silence' the Knight who 'was fond of throwing oranges at flocks of crows on moonlit nights' disappears the day after his wedding, 'the young bride's smile' does not desert her, her belly swells and, on the day she gives birth, one of the men of the alley throws 'an orange pip at the paper factory, [burning it] down and the crows were suffocated'. The children, moreover, continue to see the knight in spite of official denials of his existence.

In 'A Green House with a Brick-Red Roof' in **Shadows of Paradise Lost**, Hassan asks, '"And however will He descend from the heavens, there between those stark rocks?"' In 'Norma and the Snowman' in **Dreams of Paradise Redeemed**, Said Abu Jaber, the 'snowman' keeping a gun emplacement on a hill in the mountains, does descend, a saviour, to the group of *fedaiyin* stationed in the valley, simple, non-heroic mén, never reaching biblical proportions, but men with 'legitimate dreams'. But though a redeemer of sorts, Said too is very much a human being, one with a sense of humour, who, though a freedom fighter on duty with a *doshka*, will see a white rabbit brought into the tent to save it from freezing to death on a harsh winter night and have it freed when the weather is warmer, and who 'loves a girl called Norma', Norma, the fruit-juice seller, whose 'face and neck are freckled', 'who squeezes oranges and washes glasses, suffers from dizziness and chapped palms . . .'

And just as the inscription 'Hassan loves Zeinab' has the last word in the poignant story 'A Green House with a Brick-Red Roof' in Section I, Wadi's story 'The Grass' in Section VI ends with 'letters spelling the name of [the narrator's] beloved' – except in the latter story, it is in the first person that the name is read out. Because Hassan and Zeinab die before their story ends, the inscription at the foot of their drawing is incorporated into the omniscient point of view and thus speaks through the children's silence. On the other hand, although the narrator of Wadi's 'The Grass' staggers beneath the blows of his interrogators 'like the flame of a lantern of a deserted monastery extinguished in the winter . . . until [he] fell to the ground',

> it occurred to me to look carefully at my own arms. On one of them was a rose smiling cheerfully. And on the other, letters spelling the name of my beloved.

Recurrent themes

Needless to say, the framework into which the stories have been placed, the meta-narrative imposed on them, is inevitably a loose one. Each story is not a 'pure' example of the category into which it has been slotted. We are already in Babel, as the jagged edges of our meta-narrative testify, as soon as we tell stories. Images recur across all six sections of this anthology, points of view shift from one story to the next and within many of the stories protagonist and antagonist have a thousand and one faces ... and sometimes none.

It is not surprising that the image of the tree should figure so strongly in the literature of a dispossessed people whose society was largely agrarian. In many of the stories, such as 'A Green House with a Brick-Red Roof' and 'A Boy and Girl from Deheisha', it symbolizes rootedness, though not necessarily permanence. A post-lapsarian tree (and the story of the tree is also present in the Qur'an), it can turn sour as in Shaheen's story, its fruit is forbidden as in Badr's 'The Trellised Vine', and it may even be connected with death as in 'The Man Who Lies a Lot'. To be understood, this tree requires a historical bent of mind, a mind which can forge links between past and present as in 'At Last the Almond Blossomed'. It can be forged, fraudulently copied like the cedar tree on the Lebanese ID seal in 'A Palestinian'. Above all, however, it signifies the possibility of rebirth, as in 'Um al-Khayr' and Abu Shawer's 'The Tree'.

No less significant or powerful an image, and one that appears in many of these stories, is that of the fruit borne of trees: the sweet *gemeiz*, the shrivelled olive and, not surprisingly, the orange, which may be thrown at crows as stones are at soldiers. Oranges and olives, the fruit of a peasant's labour; children, of a woman's labour. The word *intifada*, comes from the Arabic root *n(a)f(a)d(a)*, which not only means 'to brush off' as one does with dust, but also 'to bear' as in bearing a child. Thus, not only trees and fruit, but also the image of the pregnant, fertile, *nafood* woman figures strongly in many of the stories: 'Pizza in Memory of Mariam', 'Um al-Khayr', 'The Earth' and 'The Photograph' (from 'A Land of Stone and Thyme') are some examples.

Nor is it surprising that the 'family home' should be a recurrent motif in this anthology. Samiha from Deheisha dreams of one in which she can have her own room with curtains, the boy and girl of 'A Green House with a Brick-Red Roof' dream of and draw one, and in 'Stealing Away, We Returned' and 'Dead is the Yearning', the respective narrators visit the home that once was but is no longer theirs. The 'senile old man' of 'With Both of His Hands' is denied a proper family home by his son and, instead, is condescendingly provided with a bedsit and a maid to see to his laundry.

What might be more surprising, however, is not so much the dream of home – this is after all the literature of a dispossessed people – but rather the 'homely' tone that dominates many of the stories and the fact that the homeliness comes to pervade the atmosphere of even the most unhomely of settings, that of the refugee camp. Life goes on as usual; such is the subtle nature of the form of resistance to which the reader is made to bear witness. If we did not know that the story in question is Palestinian, the family discussion in 'Kurza' about where to move could easily be mistaken for a 'normal' discussion, the way, say, an American family might discuss moving, unforced, from one neighbourhood or state to another. The tone of 'And Water Has Memory' (another of the extracts from Badr's 'A Land of Stone and Thyme'), a story set in a camp that is about to be shelled, casts an atmosphere of normality or domesticity over such war-time conditions as queuing up for water at the pump. Even in 'Norma and the Snowman', which tells the story of a young man, 'the volunteer', who has just joined a group of freedom fighters with rifles and RPJs, normality and domesticity prevail: men with names and families continue, in a camp in a bitterly cold, snowy wilderness, to drink tea together, to dream of seaside holidays and playing cards in Beirut and to discuss film stars. They care for a pet rabbit even while they transport ammunition and communicate with the outside world through a wireless. In short, what many of the stories manage successfully to achieve, is to reappropriate the domestic hearth for characters who possess no fireplaces or mantelpieces.

Reinforcing this homely, domesticizing thrust of the stories are frequent references to folklore. In 'And They Confiscated Joy in My City' the protagonist, Sheikh Nasr al-Din, also referred to as Joha in Arab folk tales and known for his wit and wisdom, himself an allusion to an Arab literary tradition, makes references to heroes and villains of early Islamic history. The ghouls, princesses and the slayer of ghouls of such folk tales are cited in 'Black Lines' and 'A Boy and Girl from Deheisha', while Hassan, Khadra and the snake of 'Um al-Khayr' themselves are modelled on stock characters from Arab folklore. At a more highbrow level of the Arabic intertext, a line with very strong Qur'anic resonances – 'a garden, a paradise beneath which rivers flow' – holds a prominent position in 'Kurza', while Salah al-Din (Saladin), the noble ruler who dealt justly with and put a stop to the Crusaders led by Richard the Lionheart, is set up as an ideal in 'Norma and the Snowman'. The stories draw not only upon Arabic folklore and a highbrow Arabic tradition of imagery, but also on a specifically Palestinian tradition. The 'salted sardine of a child', referring to the tradition in some areas of Palestine of rubbing an infant down with salt for medicinal purposes, in 'Pizza in Memory of Mariam', is among such instances. Thus, where the domesticizing tendency of some of the stories shows the characters to be very much like 'the boy or girl next door', the references to a specific tradition or intertext place them firmly within an Arabic cultural context. Both tendencies move in the same direction, namely towards the restoration of the human content to the word 'Palestinian' – a word all too often voided of such content in the media and in the popular imagination of those countries where the media is a powerful formative tool of public opinion.

The stories which fill the gap between the corporeal

existence of some six million human beings on the one hand, and their dehumanization in newspaper clippings and legal documents on the other, are themselves populated by such clippings and documents produced by antagonistic authorities. In 'Kushan Number 4: Because We Love the Land' there features a letter informing the protagonist's family 'that the Boundaries Commission has discovered that the plot of land in [their] possession is the property of the state'. In 'Pizza in Memory of Mariam' there appears a doctor's prescription, and there is one implied in 'Nothing'. In the latter there is also a newspaper clipping telling us that, 'a soldier on the border [the protagonist] had suddenly opened fire with his gun on the occupied territory'. As a result, the soldier is 'confined to a mental hospital' where he cannot, like one of the characters in 'Norma and the Snowman', assert with a note of abandon and black humour, '"My rifle is my ID."' Wadi's story 'Black Lines' abounds with documents: an ID and/or passport which the narrator does not possess, a college certificate which is as useless as the formal replies to his job applications (more documents) testify, ineffectual outlines for stories and maps that stand between him and his beloved. And though the protagonist of Azzam's 'A Palestinian' manages to procure a forged Lebanese ID at an exhorbitant price, a news item announcing the arrest of a ring of ID forgers threatens his momentary peace of mind. The 'five photos in the newspaper of five counterfeiters' are especially threatening, for even though 'newspapers sometimes trade in lies', 'they do not dress up their lies with five pictures of persons of whom you knew two'.

The photo as the document on which the production of truth stands or falls and on which self-identity is erected comes up also in Darwish's 'The Man Who Lies a Lot'. 'A simple lie,' the narrator of Darwish's story remarks, 'I told in front of a colleague of mine... The next day, the lie was published in a modest place in a newspaper of minor circulation. And before I could shake off my dismay, the same story was published in a bigger newspaper, with a wider circulation, in a more prominent place, and under a big headline. One surprise came after the other, and the story was published in all newspapers. Then, because it was attributed to a "reliable source", it was broadcast on the radio. Then, on television ... And on television, what a farce! It makes me laugh to this very day ... There, there were real pictures! This picture was enough to shake my faith in reality.'

The voice of officialdom sounds out from official documents and is manipulated, parodied and subverted in some stories like 'A Boy and Girl from Deheisha', Abu Shawer's 'The Tree', 'A Chapter from the Book of Present Days', 'The Land' and 'Breaking the Silence'. In 'A Boy and Girl from Deheisha' the children chant in their games expansionist settlers' slogans in Hebrew and, in a sort of litany, recite the torture methods to which they might be subjected should they become involved in resistance. On a lighter note, Abu Shawer's naïve 'The Tree' tells of how 'the wind, rain, clouds, little children and birds got together and made the following decision: although Nixon had land-mined the Gulf of Tonkin and wanted to burn everything, the leaves of the trees would remain green'. Further on we read: 'Word of this reached Nixon and he made a note of this in his diary, "This bird is an enemy of the free world and is on the side of the revoluntionaries." Then he issued the following order, "All birds must be killed at once in order to guarantee my return to the presidency in the next elections."' Also parodying the voice of officialdom is Rimawi's hilarious (though given the context, the invasion of Lebanon, the humour is black indeed) 'A Chapter from the Book of Present Days', which reads like the breathless voice of a sports announcer or a comic monologist. The story is a savagely ironic exposé of the reactions of heads of state and the press to the atrocities committed in Lebanon.

Akram Shareem's 'The Land' and Ghareeb Asqalani's 'Breaking the Silence' are perhaps among the most experimental of the stories in this anthology when it comes to narrative structure. Newspaper clippings, reports from UNRWA, letters, fairytales, snippets of conversations (unedited), reports from the sultan and so on are juxtaposed in a collage, providing a kaleidescopic – though by no means relativistic or unstable – perspective on the resistance tactics of a group of people to the appropriation of their history (issues of paternity and lineage in 'Breaking the Silence') and of their land (in 'The Land') by antagonistic figures of authority.

Shifting points of view within individual experimental stories like 'Breaking the Silence', 'The Land' or 'The Slope' can be seen as a feature of this anthology when it is read as a whole. The protagonist in at least nine of the short stories is a child or adolescent at school or of school age, in twelve stories he is a young man in his early twenties to late thirties (a lover separated from his beloved in four, a freedom fighter or would-be freedom fighter in four), a mature, often pregnant woman in six, a middle-aged or elderly father in six, an entire village, neighbourhood or family in four . . . all from diverse occupational and socio-economic backgrounds . . . and so on. This is in no way surprising. After all, the protagonist of a Palestinian short story, even if we were to read such stories a-prioristically as pieces of resistance literature, need not necessarily be a male guerrilla aged between sixteen and fifty, wearing a red-and-white-checked *keffiyya* and wielding a machine gun. Resistance, as the *intifada* and in fact the entire eighty years of the Palestinian resistance movement have shown, cannot afford to be sexist, classist, ageist or rigidly committed to conventional weapons.

What is perhaps more surprising is the ambiguous nature of and attitude towards the antagonist. In only three of the thirty-eight stories collected here, namely 'A Boy and Girl from Deheisha', 'The Land' and 'Stealing

Away, We Returned', is the antagonist clearly cited *ad hominem* as Zionist or Israeli. In seven of the stories, Zionists or Israeli settlers are implied only. In those seven stories, it is the machinery of Zionism (whether in the literal sense of the word 'machinery' or in the sense of the occupation bureaucracy) that plays the role of antagonist. In 'A Land of Stone and Thyme', it is planes, militias and fascists; in 'Pizza in Memory of Mariam', the bombing of a camp; in 'Dead is the Yearning', the military governor; in 'And They Confiscated Joy in My City', interrogators who emerge from 'a police car bearing some resemblance to Solomon's ring and the star of David'. In 'The Homeland', not only 'soldiers', 'guards' and 'fascists', but also the protagonist's own ineffectualness take on the role of the antagonist, and while the shadow of Israeli colonialism is cast strongly over 'Nothing', the issue at stake is a more universal one, namely, the power that psychiatry wields in determining whether or not those already designated as 'patients' are sane.

In 'Flying Carpet', the Palestinian narrator engages in a long conversation with an Israeli and neither feels comfortable with the other, but that does not necessarily cast the Israeli in the role of antagonist. If anything, he is as much a victim of the situation that breeds mistrust as his Palestinian passenger. The same is true of 'A Conversation', a story very similar to 'Flying Carpet', though in the former it is by no means clear that the 'other' seduced into conversation is Israeli. And though 'Four Colours' and 'Norma and the Snowman' place their respective protagonists within the context of armed struggle and hence implicitly set them within the context of the Zionist occupation, the two stories lack antagonists. So, if we include both the seven stories which have the machinery of occupation (rather than Israelis) as antagonists and those four stories where there is a very slight and extremely ambiguous hint that the antagonist, if antagonist he is, is an Israeli, that gives us a total of fourteen stories.

Otherwise, the antagonist runs a very wide gamut, a gamut pervaded, it is true, by the issue of power/authority and empowerment/resistance. Here are some of the many manifestations of the antagonist: 'bandits', 'the tree's new guard', 'war and warplanes', 'crows', the need to move, 'the government', 'crooked lines on a map', 'kind elderly faces', 'a Jordanian officer', authorities in general, women, fear, all governments and the press, lying, the fear of ageing, cars that drink water at the expense of sheep, a charity committee that brings shoes, a rich man living in a palace, time/forgetfulness, a heartless son, death, a snake, fickle village people afraid of a snake, Nixon, men with dragon-shaped tattoos, the sultan and the merchants.

Thus what is striking about many of these stories (and numerous other Palestinian short stories not included in this anthology) is the absence of Zionists. Perhaps this is an appropriate tactical move, a reaction to the infamous dictum 'a land without a people'. A land without a people: conversely, a people without a Zionist occupation. The equation, however, is not so simple. The occupation is there throughout the stories – they do not deny the existence of 3.5 million Jews living in Israel – but it is there as a fact of life, and not as teleogically, theologically or cosmologically inevitable. It is not a Platonic essence, a Manichean eternal evil, but rather a historical fact with an all-too-human face. Palestinians, so these stories tell, are human beings who are 'fed with the same food, hurt with the same weapons, subject to the same diseases, healed by the same means, warmed and cooled by the same winter and summer', as Shakespeare's Shylock poignantly said of the Jews centuries earlier; if pricked, they will bleed, and if tickled, they will laugh. And because their struggle is not elevated in these stories to a supra-historical realm, neither are the Israeli Jews transformed into demonic untouchables. The epic, it is true, is glimpsed every now and then in the stories, but it is almost always rooted in history and anchored in domestic detail. Above all, the stories do not demand that the reader be a Palestinian or a convert to 'the cause' to understand the experiences which they narrate; rather they appeal to a common, shared humanity.

3 Accommodating Babel:
A Note on the Politics of Translation

In the process of translating these stories, the idea was always to err on the side of literality. This intentional erring does not stem from a belief in the metaphysical notion of an 'original' or from the impossible observation of an ethical imperative to be faithful to it, but rather it is rooted in an awareness of the politics of reading in general and of reading another culture in particular. Translation, it is true, by making literatures other than one's own accessible, makes possible a cross-cultural encounter slightly more intimate than 'being there' as a tourist. But the term 'target language', which denotes the language into which the text is being translated, indicates, with its military resonance, that translation is not only about desire and intimacy, but might also involve power struggles and domination. Until very recently, the tendency in translation had been to make reading a translated text as smooth and as easy a process as possible. A text translated, say, from Arabic, should read 'as if' it had been written in English. That is, it should err on the side of the recipient's comfort and prioritize the target language.

Or so the tendency has been. But, as Lawrence Venuti points out in his introduction to *Rethinking Translation: Discourse, Subjectivity, Ideology*: 'When the target language is contemporary English, transparent discourse sustains the grossly unequal cultural exchanges between the hegemonic English-language nations, particularly the United States, and others in Europe, Africa, Asia and the Americas.'* Thus, translating from English, the politically dominant language of the late twentieth century, into a language like Arabic, Hindi, Swahili or Kurdish, is one story; translating into English is another. So it is not a question of translation 'in general', but rather of which language is being translated into which at a particular historical moment.

Instead of erring on the side of the reader, the other option in translation is to err on the side of the text. By erring on the side of literality when translating an Arabic text into English, the translator places the reader in the uncomfortable but also enabling position of being continually reminded that the literature he or she is reading belongs to another linguistic system and hence to another cultural formation. Cross-cultural encounters are not as easy, the reader is reminded, as today's new internationalist parlance attempts to convince us is the case. A non-fluent strategy of translating into English would show that Arabic writing, in this case Palestinian–Arabic writing, cannot so easily be appropriated by or naturalized and domesticated into English. It resists. A translator belonging to a cultural tradition that is not at the present time politically dominant can enable the English-speaking reader to witness this resistance. And to be in a position wherein English is defamiliarized and

*London: Routledge, 1992, p 5

27

does not read as smoothly as it does on CNN, is an enabling one indeed for the English speaker. He or she is reminded, albeit in an indirect way, that English still cannot say everything and that it has not exhausted all of its semantic possibilities – something of which poets, English-speaking or otherwise, have continually been aware when encountering their mother tongue.

To maintain their dominant positions, dominant languages are involved in long complicated processes of smoothing over the gaps and discontinuities between what is politically speaking sayable and what is indeed the case. One need but refer the reader to any media coverage of war. There is nothing, so such languages attempt to posit, outside or beyond us. In us, the end of history has arrived. 'To say anything,' a dominant language, by virtue of being dominant and in order to perpetuate its dominance, would say, 'you must speak on my terms'. For speakers of other languages to contest this monopoly of iterability, it is not enough to be elsewhere. Elsewhere is outside the arena of power struggle. Not to write in the dominant language, it is true, is to affirm alternative ones, but it is to affirm them without dictating any terms upon the dominant language and hence to let it, and the status quo, be.

This is where a non-fluent, non-transparent strategy of translation – one which does not smooth away the ragged edges of difference – can come in. One danger of such an approach is that the translated literature might sound 'exotic', and exoticizing a culture or a literature is one of the ways in which its state of being dominated is perpetuated. Another danger is that, by being retold in English, a narrative in Ibu, for example, would, in spite of its lack of fluency (or perhaps because of this very lack) find itself incorporated in the very dominant language from which it was writing itself away.

But this is the danger of any political or cultural encounter. On the one hand, it must occur on the terrain of the dominant forces – after all, that is where power lies. But, on the other hand, to speak on the terms of these forces is already to have lost the battle. This is especially the case when what is at stake is a language. The *intifada* can in many ways be read as an attempt to lure the opponent on to other grounds: instead of speaking the high-tech language of machine guns and conventional warfare, the *intifada* dictated *shared* myths involving youngsters and stones. Gandhi's passive resistence is another instance of forsaking the oppressor's terms without abdicating the struggle for empowerment.

And literature perhaps is not an either/or arena. The conflicts there, though no less real than those of the 'real' world of wars and peace accords, are more gentle and perhaps more insistent upon a common humanity and upon the possibility of games where all can partake and win. In literature, it might be possible to speak on the other's terms while at the same time dictating one's own. If translation is awake to the fact that the desire for conversation and comprehension is a desire for recognizing and respecting others, it can show how English need not necessarily operate only as the language of a new international order based on the exclusion of those to whom it does not yet make sense. English can be made other-wise, if one approaches it with respect for its differences and inadequacies, and accepts them as such. It can become aware, in the ruptures, discontinuities and awkwardness of translation, of its desire, if not for a universalist notion of humanity, then for a common space which can accommodate a Babel made less disabling and less tragic by our attempt to grapple with it.

Acknowleggements

I would like to thank my father and co-editor Abdelwahab
Elmessiri. Without his previous experience in the comp-
ilation, translation and editing of anthologies of Palestinian literature and without his encouragement, this
anthology would not have materialized.

We would both like to express our deep gratitude to
Mohamed Hesham and Ossama al-Qaffash for their
painstaking assistance in the process of anthologizing.
Thanks are due to Anni Kanafani and the Ghassan
Kanafani Cultural Foundation for granting us permission
to include in the anthology our translation of the stories
by Ghassan Kanafani, the copyright for the originals
being Mrs Anni Kanafani's sole property. As for the rest of
the stories, thanks are due to the Palestinian Writers'
Union for giving us permission to include our translation
of these stories. We are especially indebted to Ahmed
Sidqi al-Dajjani and Ahmad Omar Shaheen for sharing
with us their knowledge of Palestinian literary and folk
traditions and dialects. We would like to thank Nicholas
Crowe and Nigel Ryan who went over the English
manuscript and suggested a number of changes. Thanks
are due to Denys Johnson-Davies for his warm support of
the anthology as it passed through its many stages.

For encouragement, support and so much more –
during, before and after – it is Hoda Hegazy whom we
thank.

Nur Elmessiri
Cairo, 15 March 1996

I

Shadows of Paradise Lost

The Tree

Ahmed Omar Shaheen

'Wait for me by the ancient *gemeiz* tree near the border of our land,' he had said. 'It will shade and protect you.'

We had often played there, eating the honey-sweet fruits of the tree, concealed from the bandits. Like a mother, the tree had protected us, offering us refuge in its abundant, intertwining branches. And because the guardian of the *gemeiz* tree protected us too, we would throw stones at the bandits, and they could do nothing in return.

Our memory of the tree and of the shade beneath its trellis-like branches is ancient. But then it happened. One day the bandits joined forces. Together they tied a strong rope around the thick trunk of the tree and with red-hot irons they branded it. In the branches of the tree the birds recoiled, and many migrated, fleeing the branches. The tree was no longer the tree we remembered.

A barrier grew between us. No longer could we rest in the branches or enjoy its shade, and it seemed as though the statues scattered around the tree were kinder to us than the new guardian. The trunk grew hollow, and the branches drooped in all directions, like the arms of a decrepit octopus. Insects bored into the fruit, emerging rapacious, ugly, disgusting. Rats swarmed over the tree, and scurried among the branches.

'I'll wait at the corner,' I said.

'There you will be exposed to passers-by,' he said.

'But I will also be exposed under the tree.'

He paused for a while, then went about his task.

Translated by Nur Elmessiri

A Boy and Girl from Deheisha

Mohamed Ali Taha

I sat on an ancient olive-tree stump and began to scrub clean the plates, cups and spoons after my family had had breakfast. Sitting in the courtyard of the house like this is a part of my life. I looked up at the radiant sun whose warm autumnal rays caressed my body and I smiled. My soft hands continued playing with a plate and I hummed a tune by Marcel Khalifa. I passed my wet hands over the pair of doves on my chest and once again I looked up at the radiant sun. He had said to me, when I passed on the bottle to him, 'I'll pluck the sun and put it in your vase.' Everything yields to that boy, but most of all his tongue obeys him so, choosing splendid poetic phrases, saving me from my harsh world and instilling a new love of life in my heart. Does he know that the one vase we have at home is a very simple one I made in an arts and crafts lesson at school, and that it is not acquainted with flowers save wild ones like narcissi and anemones?

People in the camps do not buy flowers, nor do they offer them at birthdays and anniversaries. Perhaps my parents have forgotten their wedding anniversary. As for me, I do not celebrate my birthday; a birthday is a luxury that no boy or girl of the camp can afford.

When are we going to have a house? A house like others have, like those houses I see in the city, like those houses I read about in books. Why should I not have a room of my own with a bed, a pillow and a window with a curtain that I pull back in the evening to whisper sweet nothings to the silvery moon? Why can we not have a house with its own kitchen, a hot-water tap and a marble sink where I can wash the plates and cups and set them out in order?

He said to me, 'I'll pluck the sun and put it in your vase!'

He asked me, 'What does your father do?'

'He builds houses and shelters for them.'

'In Kefar Save or Tel Aviv?'

'Both. And in Kiryat Arbaa, too.'

He looked at me. I felt overcome with shame. Why, Father, should you build houses for them? They demolished my friend Nagwa's house and the house of Hassan al-Farran the baker, too. But he saved my face when he said, 'My father plants and tends their vegetables. He reaps the harvest for them, too.'

After classes were over, we played games together like 'Boys and Girls'. And we played all sorts of amusing, funny and entertaining games.

This boy knows what he's doing. He knows how to lead us. And he knows how to win our trust and love.

He said, 'Let's play "Soldiers and Patriots".'

It was a new game. We did not know it and had not heard about it. And no one objected.

He divided us into two teams, one of soldiers and the other of patriots. He was the leader of the patriots and I was the leader of the soldiers.

At the top of my voice, and with a heavy accent, I shouted, 'Clear the streets!' Then I roared like a military car. Sorry, to be exact, I produced the hissing sound of a car with a six-pointed star.

I walked on and my team followed. We sang and fired imaginary bullets. Then I shouted, 'Yerushalem?'

'Shelano.'

'Beit Lekhem?'

'Shelano.'

'Hevron?'

'Shelano.'

'Yereho?'

'Shelano.'

'L'Arabim?'

'Hamedbar.'*

The stones showered on us like a downpour of rain. We dispersed quickly and I hid behind the fence of a nearby house. I saw our friend Sami taking refuge behind the wall of one of the houses. 'Careful, Moshe. Stones are blind,' I said, pulling his leg.

'Me, I'm not scared,' he answered.

Sissy Sami was beginning to master the game. Suddenly, he screamed out in pain, 'My head, my head!'

I realized he had been hit, and I rushed over to him. Blood streaked his face in crooked red lines. When he saw me, he said, 'We said we'd play a game but Thabit made it for real.'

Whenever I run into Sami, I greet him with the following sentence, 'We said we'd play a game, but Thabit made it for real!'

*Hebrew for:
'Jerusalem?'
'Ours.'
'Bethlehem?'
'Ours.'
'Hebron.'
'Ours.'
'Jericho?'
'Ours.'
'For the Arabs?'
'The desert.'

He looks at me reproachfully. I laugh and say, 'Serves you right, you army of occupation.'

He gets furious and makes to slap me. So I run and he runs after me.

'When?' I asked him.

'When al-Shater Hassan the Clever slays the ghoul,' he answered.

When I got back home, I remembered his hair and his eyes and his nose as I made a drawing of al-Shater Hassan the Clever stabbing the ghoul in her chest!

In the corner of the picture, I drew a radiant sun and a house and . . . and . . . well I won't say. Guess what?

'If they put your feet in stocks?'

'I will not confess.'

'If they hold you under in cold water?'

'I will not confess.'

'If they give you electric shocks?'

'I will not confess.'

'If they pluck your eyelashes out one by one?'

'Ouch! I will not confess.'

'If they tear out your nails?'

'Ouch! Ouch! I will not confess.'

'If they put a stick up your anns?'

'Never, never will I confess.'

'If they use all the Savak methods?'

'I will not confess.'

'What else is there? I forget. What's left?'

He smiled and said, 'And the CIA?'

I said, 'And the CIA?'

He replied with resolve, 'I will not confess!'

I looked at the down on his chin. I imagined him bearded, like Che Guevara. I wished I could kiss him. My heart danced.

Thabit is a man.

Thabit will not confess.

And this game, I do not like it, for it is sad and desolate.

With resolve he said, 'Abla is to take care of Zone I, from the mosque to the *falafel* vendor. Samiha is to attend to the market area. Sami is to see to al-Sayyagh Street. Things have to be carried out quickly. We should avoid getting into arguments. We'll meet at ten in the square of al-Fouqa Alley. And bring your ball along, Sami!'

We rushed off.

I felt I had grown up all of a sudden. I, Samiha, daughter of Adel, a militant *fedai*, struggling against the army of occupation with its officers, soldiers, tanks, aeroplanes and rockets, to forge a new dawn. Had it not been for all the instructions and the need for discipline, I would have jumped up and down in the street and shouted, 'Down with the occupation!' I visualized the four-coloured flag looming high above the post office ... I could almost hear my classmates chanting the anthem, 'My Homeland! Oh, my Homeland!' in the schoolyard.

I went into the first shop. There were three customers. The shopkeeper is about my father's age. (My father builds houses and shelters for them, to put bread in our mouths.) The shopkeeper's white face is flushed, white hairs decorate his temples. He is elegantly dressed, his shoes as shiny as his hair. The first customer went out. 'Woollen and silken garments for ladies and gentlemen. In God we trust. No payment in instalments, no complaints. Honesty is our motto.' I smiled; he must be making a large profit. Customers do not haggle with him and his price is fixed. The second customer went out. He glanced towards me and smiled, as if he had just noticed me for the first time. Do I look as if I will be buying an expensive dress? And why shouldn't I buy that dress? It's in burgundy velvet and would suit me. Thabit! Oh, Thabit. Why should I not buy it? Buy it? I ... well. Well, why should I not afford it?

'What does the young lady desire?'

I woke from my reverie. I approached him and spoke the words in a faint whisper. He looked at me, contemplating me with anxiety or maybe happiness. But then he said, 'For the Homeland and the revolution, we are willing to stake ourselves!'

I left the shop quickly and went into the one next door. Without waiting, I whispered in the shopkeeper's ear and left before I could hear his answer. I entered, left; entered, left.

The locks were put back on the metal doors.

And I felt I was ten years older.

We waited for him at the school gate. He arrived carrying a full bag and gave out the onions. For each, an onion, and this one is for you, Samiha. A home-grown onion. The tyres are ready, Sami is to burn them. And the bullets? For those we should thank the valley. Its stones are solid and smooth. 'Aim well, my boy.' The vulnerable organs are the eyes and the area of the ear. What about the nose? I once hit a soldier on his nose and he spun round himself like a top at great speed. It was then that I remembered the astronomy teacher asking Tahsin why the earth spins around itself and his answer was, 'Because it's stupid.'

The occupation is stupid. It spins around itself. It will faint. And fall. And rain will fall and cleanse the streets. And the sun will rise and Thabit will pluck it and put it in my vase. And we will build a house with a marble sink and a room and a bed and a window and a curtain and a silvery moon.

He took off his shirt.

What a boy! He's splendid. He draped himself in the four-coloured flag, making a suit of it. He put on his shirt and walked with his head held high. He climbed the stairs. The flag flutters above the school building.

Peace be on you!

Our hearts were with him.

A car with five soldiers approached.

... According to Samiha, according to Thabit, according

to the history teacher of the Deheisha Camp Primary School who said, 'And in Ein Galouth was the end of Hulagu'. . .*

And the barricade was made of blazing tyres.

I once saw a speckled snake in the courtyard of our house. And I hid. My father looked all over the place but could not find it, so he burnt a rubber tyre. Blazing tyres drive away snakes.

The military car stopped. Two soldiers stepped out to clear the road. The stones poured down.

Let it rain, O World. Let it pour.

The bullets roared.

They broke through the wall.

They sprayed the gas.

I felt the home-grown onion in my pocket.

They closed down a school.

And opened a prison.

Beloved, Palestine is my beloved. I love you and for you I live. I burn rubber tyres and throw stones at soldiers, so that you be mine, mine alone, alone. I am yours, and you are mine. I see you in all things. In the white almond blossom and in the red anemones and in the grass, wet with the dew of dawn, and in the dark face of the shepherd . . . and in the morning star.

'Samiha, you are the Homeland!'

'Me, boy? Do you know who I am? My father builds shelters for them in Kiryat Arbaa on the land of Hebron, al-Khalil, God's beloved.' Is it true, Abraham, oh beloved of the merciful, that you are our father and theirs too? And I dream of a house with a concrete ceiling and a sink and a tap and a room and a bed and a window and a curtain . . . and a moon.

*Ein Galouth is where the Arab Muslim armies defeated the Mongols who were led by Hulagu Khan.

My lover's face, O Moon, is more beautiful than yours.

My lover is bright while you are dumb.

My lover is courageous while you are a coward.

My lover struggles against the occupation while you shine on all alike.

My lover raises the flag, burns tyres, throws stones at soldiers, gives out home-grown onions and resists tear gas.

And my lover sleeps tonight in Maskoubiyya prison.

I love you, O Palestine, and Thabit loves you. I see you, my love, as a big heart with its top in al-Matala and its base in al-Naqeb; and inside it two names embrace . . . Thabit.

Our love for you is *thabit*, steadfast.

Thabit raises the flag in the town centre. My mother ululates. The boys and girls are singing.

For yours is my love, my heart.

For yours is my love, my heart.

Letter D for destroy.

Letter H for home.

Letter C for camp.

Letter D for Deheisha.

So what did you do about it? What did you do, Mona, and you, Samira, and you, Kahdija, and you, Atef? What did you do, Ahmed, and you, Sameh, and you, Hanna, and you, Ali?

My father and yours build houses for them while they tear down our homes.

We plant flowers while they fire bullets.

And Thabit is strong and will not confess.

And we hate you, hate you, hate you, hate you.

Accursed are your mothers.

I now know how to transform a bottle into a molotov cocktail.

Bullets are not to be met with flowers.

Nor is a tank to be met with a lily.

I sat on an ancient olive-tree stump and began to scrub clean the plates, spoons and cups.

A bird chirped and the sun caressed my neck.

He said to me, 'I will pluck the sun and put it in your vase.'

A military car arrived. A soldier pounced on me, wrapped my hair around his fist and dragged me to the car.

Vandal.

Fatah.*

Whore.

And you dare throw Molotov cocktails at cars?

A terrible light blazed in the room. With an unconscious gesture, Samiha's mother passed her hand over her eyes. She saw the sun like a yellow orange falling into her daughter's vase and setting at her door.

Translated by Hala Halim

*al Fatah the Palestine National Liberation Movement   PNLM

A Green House with a Brick-Red Roof

Rashad Abu Shawer

When they were outside the gate, they looked at each other affectionately, smiled, held out their little arms and clasped each other's fingers. They hopped about, first on one foot, then the other, shaking their heads like two happy sparrows. They came to the foot of al-Tajruba Mountain, the Mountain of Trials and there, on the dirt path leading to al-Dayouk Spring, they drew a rectangle, which they divided into squares, took a flat pebble and began to play hopscotch ... leaping, panting, laughing.

Hassan leapt up twice, then stopped, and let his leg down to rest next to the other leg. He said to the little girl whose name was Zeinab, 'Are you tired?'

'Come, let's sit there,' she said, pointing with little fingers at the palm tree under which they used always to sit whenever they had tired themselves out.

He leapt about, putting one foot down and lifting the other, wide leaps, and then, throwing his body in the air, he rolled on the green expanse of grass. As for her, she was moving slowly, looking at him, a smile quivering like a butterfly on her sweet lips.

She stretched beside him on the grass. The water was flowing in a little ditch, watering the field. He dipped his head in and wet his neck, and then, scooping up some water in both of his palms, he sprinkled it on her. She drew back, squealing coquettishly. But once again he sprinkled

43

her, wetting her dress which then clung to her shoulders.

'You've soaked me.'

'Ha ha ha!'

'My mother will beat me.'

'If she beats you, I'll buy a knife and creep up to your house at night and slay her.'

Zeinab put her hands over her eyes and started crying.

'Why do you want to kill her? Do you want me to live without a mother?'

He came close to her, brought her head to his breast and rocked her.

'No . . . I won't kill her . . . I'm just teasing.'

'You won't buy a knife, will you?'

'I won't buy a knife.'

'And you wouldn't think of killing my mother even if she beat me?'

'Even if she beat you,' he said, 'and beat me too . . . I would love her for your sake.'

They put the drawing pad down on the grass in front of them and took out bits of coloured crayons from their pockets. Their fingers pressed the crayons on to the paper, making a soft squeaking sound. They drew a green and red house. The walls were green. As for the roof, it was red, the brick-red colour covering the roofs of the houses in Jericho. Beneath the house, Hassan wrote: 'This is the house of Hassan and Zeinab.'

'We should make a fence out of trees for the house.'

With the green, they drew many orange trees on which there were many oranges.

'And this,' she said, 'is a palm tree because you love the palm tree under which we sit.'

'And this,' he said, 'is a bird with yellow feathers.'

And when they were done drawing the bird, they heard a sweet chirping sound.

'Ah, how beautiful,' they said in unison.

And they looked in each other's eyes and laughed.

'But where will our house be?' she asked.

'I don't know,' he said. 'You will live with us, my family and me, in our village.'

'But I'm young and my family might not let me leave them.'

'And I too am young and my family might not let me leave *them*.'

She folded her head beneath her arms and she seemed like a lonely dove. He rested his head against the trunk of the palm tree; his features had changed.

He called to her but she sobbed and did not reply. Scooping up some water, he washed her face and stroked her hair. Then he tapped on her nose with his finger and a beam of light shone on her lips. And her face had become an orange washed with dew.

'The teacher,' he said, 'told us we'd return to our homes.'

'The teacher said,' she said, 'that we'd return to our homes. And then she dismissed us.'

'But then we'd part,' he said, 'and if we go back there, I won't see you any more.'

The girl drowned in silence. He took her by the hand, tucked the drawing pad under his arm, stuffed the crayons into her dress pocket and they walked very close to each other. He said, 'But I'll grow up and I'll come to your family home and take you . . .'

'And if you forget me?'

'How could I forget you?'

And to draw her out of her silence and sorrow, he asked her, 'And however will He descend from the heavens, there between those stark rocks?'

'I don't know,' she said. 'But why is His house between those rocks?'

They heard a shrill sound passing above them. They saw a huge fire rearing its head up at the Castle of Hisham Ibn Abd al-Malik.* They were frightened. They began to run.

*one of the Umayyad caliphs

'War has come,' he said to her.

Breathing unsteadily, she said, 'I'm scared.'

He pressed her hand, 'Don't be scared. I am with you.'

They ran faster. The shrill sounds were passing above them ... their heads rolled and then settled side by side ... they were like two wilted oranges ... their flesh clung to the trees. The crayons were scattered and the paper on which was drawn a green house with a brick-red roof was blown away.

Hassan loves Zeinab.

Translated by Nur Elmessiri

The Bird

Farouk Wadi

Our village did not know love. Only flocks of pitch-black crows had circled in its skies. One day, when I was still a child, I drew near my father and asked, 'Father, do you know love?'

For a long time my father wept. The tears fell from his eyes, steady and pure, and his face overflowed with an old grief. He told me stories of an ancient love. And then, mother came and wept, listening to Father's words. And I, I too wept.

One smiley-sun day, love came to our village, a colourful bird. He sang with a voice the likes of which we had never known before. We beheld him that day with wonder and longing. We listened to him attentively, and with quivering joy.

And that day, the people of the village gained many years.

The children of the village, its men, its women, its elderly, all of them knew love. And had your eyes visited us that day and wandered in the streets of the village, they would have seen hearts fluttering everywhere, racing in the streets, full of joy, full of greenery.

But when night, a dark sea, washed over our village, things were submerged into cruel darkness and people felt as though something were crushing them.

Through the twilight of dawn and fires, we crept about

in the village streets. We could not hear the sound of the bird that had sung in our sky. We were struck with a painful grief, as our eyes circled the sky in search of the bird, and the flock of night crows appeared. They circled above our heads, drawing terrible shapes.

Translated by Nur Elmessiri

II

Exile from the Land

Kurza

Rasmi Abu Ali

Summer passed and the gaze of the elders was turned towards the village, waiting for the miracle. But the miracle did not happen and September came, bringing with it the chilly night air, and the shacks we had built out of branches were strewn everywhere.

'Well, folks, what is to be done?'

Some relatives, without further ado, simply went to Bethlehem, getting a truck to move them. Others preferred to migrate to nearby Beit Jala.

As for us, we remained, turning the matter over in our minds, considering it from all angles. It was autumn and the elders had to decide quickly, for winter would be coming soon.

Finally, they held a general meeting to seek a course of action. It was attended by young and old.

'Let's go to Bethlehem as our relatives did,' Uncle Gadallah said. 'Or to Beit Jala as Uncle Abu Sidqy suggested. Then, when we get back the village, we will at least be close to it,' he added.

Sheikh Issa remained silent, his head bowed, hugging his cane. His fez, always upright, was askew.

'What do you say, Sheikh Issa?'

Sheikh Issa replied as if he had prepared his suggestion a long time ago, 'I say we go to Kurza.'

'Where?!' everyone cried out in unison.

'For God's sake, calm down.'

'But to Kurza, Sheikh! Have mercy on us!'

'Calm down, I say. You've got to give and take, good people. Or don't you want anyone to speak their mind?'

The uproar died down and the Sheikh went on, 'When Sheikh Farhan and his people came to visit us, we spared no expense, our hospitality kept the butcher busy. Isn't that so?'

'True . . .' some murmured.

'But . . .'

'What I'm saying is if we went to our kinsmen and friends, they'd take good care of us, I'm sure. Sheikh Farhan and Sheikh Mobarak are considered true sheikhs back in their village. We would stay with them till things began to look up; and, God willing, it won't take long till they do. By early spring, things will have taken shape. I say we go there till things look up.'

'But it's so far away, Sheikh. We have indeed heard of it, but no one has ever seen it.'

'As for distance, it is immaterial if we go by car. Twenty or thirty kilometres south of Galilee and we'd be there.'

'Then it's close to Zahria?' one of those present asked.

'My good fellow, it's before Zahria. Between Galilee and Zahria . . . satisfied?'

'Does it have trees and greenery?'

'A garden, a paradise, a paradise beneath which rivers flow.'*

'You can't be serious.'

'A paradise, I say, beneath which rivers flow – a land of plenty. The orchards are orchards. The vineyards vineyards. And the water there gushes forth like a river.'

No one dared remind Sheikh Issa he was blind. How, then, could he have seen all these paradises? Could anyone have dared?

*This line very explictly echoes Qur'anic imagery and idiom.

To cut a long story short, that evening Kurza seemed to everyone to be paradise or the promised land. So they agreed without hesitation to go there.

And, that night, everyone went to sleep dreaming of the promised paradise, Kurza.

Translated by Karaz Mona Hamdy

Stealing Away, We Returned

Rasmi Abu Ali

The snow melted; the rain ceased. A kind of blackish-brown worm began crawling about everywhere. Mother remarked, 'The burning coals have all fallen. Winter is past.'*

It had been a harsh winter indeed, as if nature had formed an alliance with the catastrophe that had befallen us.

'Of course,' some people said. 'People have forgotten God. So what has happened had to happen.' And people began to believe that God had sent them such punishment only because they deserved it.

Almonds bore blossom in the valley; gardens blazed with the colour white; yellow blossoms and anemones burst into copious flower, so that the land around the house was covered. I ran with the other children, carrying a twig sling and tirelessly chasing birds. It was as if we had never left al-Malha. The place is the place, and the smell of the earth is the smell of the earth. The tiny fissures in the rocks, gurgling with sweet water, are the same, so too are the holes out of which the snails stick their necks cautiously, and the herds of braying donkeys, stuffing

---

*According to folk tradition in Palestine, three burning coals fall during the winter. Winter is over when the third one falls.

their bellies with fresh grass. And yet, something was missing from it all. I wonder what that thing was?

April ended; May began. The weather became hot. Someone came to tell my mother that some al-Malha people were stealing into al-Malha like thieves in the night to carry away some odds and ends, and that yet others were going to the olive groves to gather the olives that had fallen to the ground.

'But the Jews, do they allow this?'

'There's no one there in the village, not even a sparrow.'

The next morning, my mother asked me to go with her. We set off early and I carried her large straw basket. We knew the way westwards through the olive groves surrounding Bethlehem. Cutting across the olive groves, we approached Shurfat village to the right. From there, we looked down on the valley through which the railway tracks ran. A year had passed since the land was deserted. Wild grass, as tall as a man, had sprung up.

My mother surveyed everything mournfully. Tears fell from her eyes as she said, 'See what happens to the land, my son, when its people desert it?'

We could see the eastern section of the village, but it was enveloped in some sort of black cloud. A cloud of desolation or was it a real cloud? We moved on down the slope. The old path had disappeared, so we pushed through the high sea of grass. When we reached the railway tracks we came up against some barbed wire and with some difficulty we crossed it. When we arrived, we found many of the women already there, searching for the lost olive harvest.

How strong the force of habit and the sense of property! Although the valley was overgrown with olive trees, each woman, we noticed, did not trespass on another's patch, but gathered only from her own. This, in spite of the fact that they had been dispossessed of the land and all that was on it.

We headed towards our trees at a place called al-Najma.

I knew each of the trees well since the days when, during the harvest, we were given three days' holiday from school in order to help our families gather in the crop.

We rummaged through the damp dust in search of olives. Most of them were shrivelled and bad; yet we were able to fill the basket. We were afraid; we kept our eyes the whole time on the dirt path running parallel to the railway tracks where Jewish patrols, it was said, occasionally passed.

Mother gathered together her harvest of shrivelled olives, and we rushed back.

Two days later, mother was keen to go into the village to bring back the clothes we had left behind in grandfather's house.

'You are pushing your luck,' father said.

But she insisted, and we went back the following morning.

We found some women gathering olives. We asked if anyone had gone into the village, and a woman replied that many had gone, meeting nobody along the way for the village was deserted.

We continued our journey across that overgrown meadow, groping for a way through with difficulty.

Presently, we found ourselves at the beginning of the alley leading to my grandfather's house.

It was absolutely silent and I could hear my heart beating like a drum. What if a Jewish soldier came across us? He would kill us on sight.

But there was no one there. We arrived at the ground floor and, without delay, mother began to collect some clothes, putting them in the bag she was carrying. Myself, why I could not say, I began to collect empty bottles.

'What do we need those empty bottles for?' Mother scolded. 'Go and look for clothes – that's what we need.'

I didn't look for clothes, but instead gathered some schoolbooks, including the Qur'an, which I put in the basket. Then I found a broken serving spoon which I added to my precious booty.

Before carrying away our things, I thought that I should like to see the upper part of grandfather's house. I climbed the stone steps and when I reached the upstairs rooms, I found a huge hole in the ceiling. Winter had left its mark on everything inside. It must have been a bomb that made the hole.

We hurried back, mother groaning beneath the full bag, I carrying the basket full of books and the broken serving spoon. Approaching the railway tracks, we stopped to rest, putting down our loads near the women gathering olives. I noticed for the first time the presence of an old man. He too was bent over, gathering olives.

Suddenly, a patrol appeared on the road. The soldiers saw us immediately, and one of them fired at us with a machine gun installed on the back of an army truck. The old man ran away, taking cover among the trees. We simply froze, knowing that our time had run out.

The soldiers approached. They had with them a blonde girl convulsed with laughter. One of them, holding a machine gun, finger on trigger, gestured to us to come nearer. We inched forward until the soldier was above our heads and we were on the other side of the tracks.

'You. What you do here?' He spoke in broken Arabic.

A woman told him that we were gathering the dry olives to eat.

'This is not your land. This Israel land.'

A second woman, emboldened by the discussion, said, 'But this is our land, foreigner.'

The soldier got angry and repeated, 'I tell you, this Israel land. You, go. Come back, I shoot. Understand?' And he fired a shot in the air.

If you escape this one, I said to myself, then come what may, you'll take everything in your stride.

When we crossed the barbed wire, I felt reborn.

Translated by Nur Elmessiri

The Land

Akram Shareem

In memory of the demolition of Qalqiliya and the battle of al-Karama

Two snippets of conversation overheard in a town preparing to fight

'Don't speak ill of the people who left their homes in June. You don't know how they thought things would end up. You didn't lose anything. You didn't race through the fields with the women and children under cover of night. We were desperate for weapons.'

'No one leaves the land . . . That is all I know. Take the people of Qalqiliya, for example.'

A story, unedited, in a town teeming with migrants

'What can I say. When they asked us to gather at the mosque the news spread among us like an order not to be questioned. The people came out of their homes, reluctant and bewildered, the men behind their wives, feeling their necks in anticipation of death, the children clinging on to the grown-ups, everyone carrying what they could, bundles and belongings.

'It was late afternoon; our eyes which hadn't seen sleep for days took in the armed Zionists who barked orders at us incessantly, in a mixture of archaic Arabic and

Hebrew. I had heard it a long time ago, in the days when the bastards used to be afraid of our children. Don't you remember? In the old days our youngsters used to terrify the Jews.

'And to keep a long story short, the buses and the trucks came and gathered in the centre of Qalqiliya, forming what seemed an endless line. The soldiers ordered us to get on . . . just like that, without a word, without any farewells . . . without us knowing where we were going.'

'Did you ask them?'

'We asked them . . . their faces weren't strange to us, we'd known them for a long time . . . we said, 'Where are you taking us?' Their tongues never stopped giving orders and they answered us only by shoving and pushing, "Get on! . . . Don't look behind! . . . Don't talk! . . . Quickly!"

'We got on.

'I got on, me and little Mahmoud and Aisha in one bus, and my wife, Um al-Iyal* with the rest of the children and her niece in another. I forgot to tell you but we had been ordered to leave everything in its place on the ground. Even the blankets and the children's clothes remained on the ground. Everything on the land, the orders said, had to remain with the land. Some of the homes in Qalqiliya, as you may well know, even had fridges and washing machines. Everything remained behind. People could have stolen anything they wanted that day.

'I'll be brief. We were crammed inside, one on top of the other, as the buses took us away from the town. There weren't even enough seats for all the women. The children were on top of them and the men squeezed together. Between the gaps in the crowd I could see Aisha's head as she clung to my knee, and her brother Mahmoud hanging on to her dress, holding it in his

---

*Um al-Iyal literally means 'the mother of the children'. It is used as a term of respect.

mouth, legs all around him. It just made me worry more about my wife, Um al-Iyal, and the rest of the children.

'We whispered to one another . . . I wonder what they're going to do with us? Where are they taking us? They've occupied the town, and us – what do they want us for?'

'Were there many buses?'

'As for me, I was in the tenth bus of the first lot. I couldn't work out how many were behind us. But I tell you, everyone, every single one of us, they crammed in like that and made off.

'What can I say?

'We became more afraid when it got dark and night fell and the buses left the paved road and turned on to a wide open plain. We couldn't see where the bus was going through the windows and we didn't know where we were heading for or in which direction they were taking us. They knew our land very well.'

'The women?'

'A girl crammed in at the back of our bus fainted. We had no water to sprinkle on her so we opened all the windows. There were cries of, "Move your heads away, let her breathe." Her father dragged her by the head to the window and I don't know what happened to her after that.

'Enough of these small details.

'Afterwards, the buses stopped in a place we didn't know; it was night. The Jews got off and walked round the buses carrying their weapons and torches and motioned to us to get off quickly. It was only then that we realized that all those lines of buses had not been enough to take all the people in one go and so they had to return for the others.

'So we got off.

'What's the point of telling you about it if you weren't there? We got off shouting one another's names, each family trying to reassemble itself in spite of the shoving and pushing. The ground was hard and dry, dusty and full of clumps of scattered summer cacti. This we found out when the soldiers ordered us to sit down, each one right where he was. I felt the ground underneath me and whispered to Um al-Iyal and the children to come closer. I sat leaning on a rock. After a little while, the order not to speak was given.

'The soldiers' figures – and, by the way, they weren't all soldiers; in fact, some of them were in civilian clothes and armed – their figures were distant and hardly visible. We couldn't feel their presence except when, from time to time, they pointed their torches at us. I tried hard to see who was around me, and who was behind me but it took a while for my eyes to get used to the dark. Gradually, my eyes made out scattered bunches of people spread out like phantoms around us. Um al-Iyal stuck close to me and I felt reassured that she was watching the children because the night had just begun.'

'Didn't you ask them?'

'I don't think anyone asked them why we'd been moved. We knew they wouldn't tell us. They might even kill those who asked. So we didn't ask, we just pictured the weapons that were pointed at us and that would remain so all night. After about an hour the order to sleep came.

'The few nervous whispers that had been our only source of comfort and reassurance disappeared, and we could hear nothing but the sharp and incessant chirping of the crickets.

'My wife leant over and asked me about the rest of Qalqiliya. I didn't know if the rest would come to the same place or not but, truly afraid, I whispered, "Thank God there aren't too many young men with us. Even if they kill all of us, at least the young men will have got away."

'What can I say?

'I stayed awake for a long time until I could no longer resist the sleepiness that had been weighing heavily on me for days. My wife, the children and the rest of the people did the same. I slept with two heads in my lap but I didn't know at the time which of my children they were.

'With the first light of day, people's heads started rising up every once in a while, glancing at one another and trying to find out where we were. As for the rest of the people of Qalqiliya, we never heard the commotion of their arrival in a second batch. We became certain that the Zionists had taken them to another place. God protect the oppressed!

'After a few minutes whistles blew; the soldiers came over pointing their machine guns and ordered us to stand up. We stood, each of us wiping his eyes and stretching his stiff body, looking at the faces of the people around him, searching in secret for his relatives.

'And as we stood there like that, the Jews screamed at us, "Go . . . Get a move on! . . . Get lost! . . . Just go . . . Anywhere you like."

'They indicated to us the direction of Amman and began to shove and push and kick, screaming in our faces: "Move! . . . Get lost! . . . Quickly! . . . Out of here . . ."

'Where do we go?

'What, please tell us anyone, can we do?

'After the Zionists had herded us a few metres towards the East Bank we stopped and watched them get into their cars and drive off.

'We remained on our own. People asked, crying, "Where do we go? Where is everyone else?" . . . There were no cars and we were dying of hunger and thirst. The children's crying and the women's sobbing seemed without end. Our faces were white, frozen with fear. I scarcely recognized Um al-Iyal from the tears and the dust and the look of fear and of terror in her eyes.

'Frankly, I just took her by the hand and we dragged the children along, and I said, "From here, to the East Bank. We have a relative who works abroad, who has a large salary and God won't forget us." I don't know what the others did that day, or where each family went. Nor do I know who found their relatives and who didn't.'

Part of an unimportant news item

20 June 1967 – News Agencies: Israeli forces are carrying
out the demolition of homes in the town of Qalqiliya on
the West Bank of the Jordan and forcibly evicting the
Arab inhabitants. The Arab states have asked the
Security Council to investigate these actions and to order
Israel to cease the evacuation of Arab inhabitants and the
demolition of their homes.

The agencies added that Israel has used all kinds of
mines and explosives to destroy the houses and remove
all traces of the town's existence.

The Arab states informed the Security Council that
around 20,000 of the town's inhabitants were still living
in the open on the hillsides and fields without shelter,
clothing or food. They also . . .

**The beginning of a long letter not delivered
by mail**

20 April 1968

Dear Ahmad,

I will talk to you at length this time. First of all I would
like to congratulate you on the feeling of anguish you
described to my cousin who was visiting you. It's a feeling
that has begun to haunt every Palestinian when people
see him and realize he isn't a *fedai*. This anguish could
mean that more people will begin to join the ranks of the
freedom fighters. Many of our new comrades have talked
about this feeling and about its effect on them.

As for the news you requested, the people left al-
Karama camp a few days before the last clashes. Your
relatives were with them, of course. They left the camp
deserted except for the *fedaiyin*, and a barber's shop and a
small grocer's to sell the men what they needed.

Imagine, tens of thousands of them in the streets, on the
pavements and in the doorways. Your sister and her
husband Mahmoud and our uncle Adel's entire family,

and others I don't know, chose to move together to the outskirts of the town. Abu Bashir promised he would secure three tents for them as soon as possible.

As for the rest of the people, they returned to Qalqiliya with most of the inhabitants who had been moved out in buses by the Jews. They didn't move to the East Bank; they witnessed none of the abuse that greeted us. And you know, they're all still alive. They've won. They and every other West Banker who stayed on his land.

I think you should know their story. After the houses had been demolished and the town ploughed into the ground, they returned. Every family sat in the place where their house had been, and they became neighbours once again. They became the townsfolk of Qalqiliya in spite of everything. They stayed there till tents were brought to them, and then set up a camp in place of the town. Each family set up its tent poles where its old house had been.

Everyone who stayed in the West Bank retained his honour and self-respect.

The advice and the will of an old peasant on the West Bank

I am an old man now. I gather in my mind three generations just as I gather all the deeds of the Zionists over the past seventy years. I have witnessed the revolution and the battles and I have heard recently of the June war. We have lived its moments here in great tension. We have been with the Zionists for twenty years. We see them night and day and we know exactly what they want; we know everything. So my advice to you is not to believe a single thing you are told. The Zionists want only the land, and they do nothing but attempt to get hold of the land, and they plan nothing but to acquire the land, as much of the land as possible. Look at how confused they are about us, we who remained on the land. They don't know what to do with us. We can see them. They are

confused about how to deal with us. We are their problem.
Our mere existence irritates and terrifies them. As if we
are an army that grows and cannot be conquered. And, for
twenty years, they have been unable to find a way to get
rid of us. We are proud of that. And they will not find a
way to get rid of an entire people.

This now is my will. The fruit of my seventy years, I
leave to every single one of you, for those present to
deliver to those absent: when the Zionist fights you, then
above everything else, remember your land.

Translated by Anthony Calderbank

Kushan* Number 4:
Because We Love the Land

Mohamed Naffaa

It seems that the letter I am going to tell you about shortly was hiding in the postman's bag, waiting its turn like the rest of the letters. We had been up since daybreak because it was spring, and the silver rays of the sun spilled on to the mountain tops and came in through the open windows, making you feel that you were still in need of sleep or wanting to lie awake in bed for a while. The field, however, demands otherwise, and my father gets up before dawn.

Out in the street everything in the village was awake and the camels, loaded up with hay, were already making their way back from the fields to the threshing area, to unload and then return. The chickens and pigeons were picking up the seeds that had fallen on the road and pecking busily at the cowpats and the camel dung. My father, striding ahead of us, was looking at the surrounding fields as if he were responsible for their harvest. 'The barley is short here; the land was muddy when they planted, you can see from those seedlings over there.' He looked over the fence and continued, 'Oh dear . . . the water has washed the soil away!' And because he kept

Kushan is the Turkish word for certificate or official document.

looking here and there, he kept walking off the road, bumping into the branch of one of the almond or olive trees planted by the earth walls on either side of the road, making the dew drops fall on my face, because I was walking right behind him, trying to follow exactly in his footsteps. He would take care for a little while and mutter, only to repeat his blunder again, until eventually we reached the field. He made his way to the large thorny tree which formed a hedge around our land and, pushing it quickly aside, we entered. The birds flew up from the olive trees in the middle of the field and landed elsewhere. He looked at my brother, who had been walking alongside me and was watching the birds wistfully: the matter was more serious than he imagined. Without more ado, my father took his jacket off and my mother put the provisions and the bucket of water under the fig tree and ... work began.

'Get those goats off the crops and come here!'

The goats and their kids were scattered over the reaped land and began to scratch about for green grass and ears of wheat. The field stretched out before us, yellow and vast, the ears of wheat leaning their heads to the east. The stalks were damp and soft, not easily broken, but as the day advanced and the sun's rays grew warmer and brighter, they dried out and the breeze blew through them, making them sway, and I heard them rustle. Colourful butterflies fluttered quietly above the ears of wheat, alighting on the mulberry bushes, whose blue flowers rose above the stalks of wheat, and moving their wings slowly. My younger brother was following them with his eyes, using any excuse to look round, to walk here and there and avoid the hard work. He was complaining about lessons and homework, the end of which he could not see, and of the shortness of the holiday. Whenever he got a chance, having made sure that my father was absorbed in his work and could hear nothing but the sound of his scythe, he would lean his head towards me and say, 'Our father exploits us during the school holidays.' Saqr (my brother) would take my reply to the protests made on behalf of the two of us as a sign of my servility to my father and, because I worked by his side all day (so my brother's accusations would go), I was never outstanding in school like him.

For me, at thirteen, and three years older than my brother, things are completely different . . . I find great pleasure working in the field with my father and mother, who are in their middle years. I would spend long hours among the green olive trees and the hanging vines heavy with unripened fruit, listening to the birds whistling and the nightingales singing, and my heart would fill with joy. And even though I disagree with my brother's point of view, I do, at the same time, have a great affection for him and cannot bear to be parted from him.

Some goats and sheep on the road were peering over the hedgerow, bleating softly as they looked at the appetizing field, at the green grass and at our animals grazing happily. But the strong thorny barrier meant they were stuck on the road. As for our animals, they did not trouble themselves except to cast swift glances to see who was calling, before returning to their grazing.

And when Saqr suggested a new way of harvesting (it makes sense to cut circles in the yellow field), my father's silence and lack of objection were encouraging, so I went and joined my brother at work. I found my father's explanation both simple and convincing. In reply to my mother's protests, he said, 'The important thing is that they reap, not how they do it. And that the wheat they are pulling up doesn't return to take root in the ground. What is required is that they reap.' All my mother said was, 'They're little devils; they are simply taking after you.' The argument ended and we moved further and further away, making trails in the fields.

Because we were working so hard, with everyone acknowledging this, and especially my father, we felt tired as we returned to the village, and I felt hungry. One meal is not enough for a long hard June day, but it is the custom of the village people to eat only once in the field.

The sun was about to set behind the high mountains when we reached the village, where the hustle and bustle at sunset was just the same as in the morning. Lines of people were moving along the road with their animals and the small children were waiting for their mothers who had spent the day in the field. As soon as one of them reached the edge of the village, a child would run up and tug at her hem or force her to carry him home at her breast, the child protesting at her absence during the day, and she adjusting his clothes and cleaning his face with her hand.

The postman came in as if he had an appointment with us. He handed my father the envelope and asked him to sign the receipt. I used to feel very important whenever we got a letter. My father handed it to me and listened closely as I unfolded the letter and began to read:

We would like to inform you that the Boundaries Commission has discovered that the plot of land in your possession is the property of the state, since it was previously woodland belonging to the state. This order will be considered in effect from the date of your receiving this notice. Any violation will render you liable to prosecution. Note: You may appeal within two months of the date of receipt.

I expected my father to show more interest in the matter and I regretted that I had read aloud and in such an official tone the letter, which was written in clear script and in classical Arabic. I think I even flinched a little under my father's mocking expression.

'Fine, then we'll learn the trade of beggars, just as they want.'

My father began to think in silence, but then people

began to pour into our house, dressed in their night clothes, waving pieces of paper in their hands. Some were cursing, some laughing raucously, yet others spoke solemnly.

My mother found consolation in other people's afflictions.

My father said, 'I can't believe it. Does the paper have my full name? Look carefully!'

When I told him that the name was correct, he turned away, furious, 'Are we going to leave the land this easily?'

'Hmm! Government!' someone cried.

'A load of rubbish!' And for the first time a slight glimmer shone in my father's eye.

'How sweet of you, government, to take Khaluit al-Nimr!' That was the name of the piece of land. 'Woodland?' he said. 'The meadow of Ibn Amer was woodland and the people reclaimed it.'

Night came with a full moon, the stars shone, and the fireflies darted here and there. The night was heavy and my father turned quietly on his bed, thinking that we had dozed off. But I could not sleep either; I kept thinking of the field in which we had planted everything, and of my mother coming back from the hillside with a heavy load of dry wood on her head, sweat pouring from her forehead and her lips dry with thirst. The heat of the sun rose from the baked earth but, despite this, each time she would drag a branch of the thorny tree to put against the fence for fear of any harm befalling the animals. I thought of my father collecting small stones and pebbles from the ground, lifting the hem of his *qumbaz* to carry them in and then laying them on the wall. And I thought of me, and of my brother Saqr, picking the ears of wheat before they turned yellow and making them into bundles, ready for *freek* to be made of them.*

---

*a dish made of roasted green wheat

And when, contrary to my usual habit, I woke up early in the morning, my father was already dressed, active and exuberant as usual. He went to wake my brother in order to go off to the field.

'Where have you put the letter?' someone asked my father as we walked along the road to the harvest.

'In hell . . . may God keep you away from it.'

'Why are you going to the field?' another said in jest. 'The field is gone.'

My father answered, clearly and with confidence: 'Because we love the land.'

Translated by Anthony Calderbank

III
Refugees in Hostile Cities

Extracts from
A Land of Stone and Thyme

Liana Badr

For two hands of stone and thyme,
this anthem is dedicated
Mahmoud Darwish, 'Ahmed al Zaatar

The Photograph

Last night I dreamt that we walked together. He always visits me in my dreams. We were walking near the martyrs' cemetery. No sooner had I seen him than he left me and went under. Just leapt down and went among the graves. He tore his photo off one of the tombs, and went off I don't know where. I looked around. I saw the graves with their white tombstones, with wreaths of dry flowers on them and, around them, spring grass, green and soft. I looked for him but didn't know where he'd gone.

The photo is on my mind. I couldn't believe it till the photographer developed it. I thought I'd go and place it on his grave in the martyrs' cemetery. But the situation is tense and the fighting is on. Who these days would dare to go down to the martyrs' burial ground? I discussed it for a long time with my sister, Jamila. But she took the enlarged photo from me, stuck it in a cupboard and locked it up. She said that I was pregnant, that I was due to deliver by the end of the month, and that it would be difficult for me to run if I got caught in the shooting. What am I to do

75

then? Wait? Life has been nothing but waiting upon waiting, even though I never did expect one day to marry a man who loves me, longs for me and waits with me and who then goes away for ever and never returns.

They used to call him 'the Indian' in al-Damoor Camp. When I first set eyes on his dark features and black eyes, I really took him for an Indian. The first time we spoke with one another, I asked him, 'Are you an Indian?' He laughed so long he almost fell flat on his face.

'Me? Indian? Yusra, I come from the village of Jamaeen on the outskirts of Nables.'

Later on, he loved to remind me of how I'd fallen for the joke and had really taken him for an Indian.

Al-Damoor

After our exodus from Tel al-Za'tar, we lived for nearly a year in al-Damoor. Our house, situated on the roadside, was dismal: no windows, or doors, or tiles, or sanitation. It was a big house, burnt from the inside, and, like the rest of the al-Damoor houses, its tiles were ripped out and its floors were sand and gravel. The first thing we did was clean it. We spent about a week cleaning it. My mother had a go at whitewashing it with lime, but it was thick with soot and grime. We got some empty ammunition boxes, the wood of which my brother used to make a front door. The windows we covered up with plastic sheets.

At night the wind would blow. We were near the sea, facing it. Mother would stay up all night, too frightened to sleep. The wind would beat against the plastic sheets and would bang against the transparent oilcloths, making sounds like the bombing. She went on feeling jittery and frightened. She was afraid in the winter and afraid in the summer. Only mother alone was afraid.

When the Israeli planes started bombarding us, my mother's nerves got so frayed that we could no longer stay in al-Damoor. Life was so hard and harsh there. The distances between houses were too great for us who had been used to living among many neighbours. The shop was far away and the vegetable market was further still. There was no running water in the house. Eventually we managed to stretch an electric wire from the main street lamp, on which we hung a bulb inside the house. But mother was always frightened and we did not like al-Damoor. We left, and moved into one of the flats in Beirut abandoned by those who had fled the fighting.

And Water Has Memory

During the last attack on the refugee camp, I was out getting water. At the last stronghold they attacked and took from us, there was a water tap. Throughout the siege, Jamila and I used to go daily to the bottom of the alley leading to al-Dikwana. The most we could ever get were two large cans of water. The water would be cut off from early morning till the afternoon or evening. We would spend eight or ten hours waiting for our turn at the tap. Sometimes we managed to get our turn; at other times the attack would begin. Bombs would shower down upon us and the water would be cut off before anyone could fill a thing.

In the beginning – the beginning of the siege – we used to fill up at the Djanin School, near the George Matta metalworks. We used to sleep in the wide vault that was the George Matta factory. The place would fill up with more than seven hundred people who shared it with pieces of metal and huge machines. We would spread the bedding between the closely stacked bars and the cutting, smelting and plumbing equipment. There was hardly any room for us amidst the heaps of chairs, beds and metal swings, all piled one on top of the other. We couldn't get any sleep for the metal and its stink. Whenever we tried to sleep, the smell of metal would get up our noses and stifle our breath.

In George Matta we remained for nearly a month. It was a dangerous site because of its proximity to the

Monastery of the Good Shepherd. Every day the women swept and sprinkled water on the floor of the factory. They did their baking on a tin tray placed on a kerosene primus. People baked and kneaded and slept and rose inside the shelter. During the first days we were able to go out sometimes to fill sandbags and to put up fortifications inside the camp. Even my mother, who had just had a baby, went out with the other women, a month after her delivery, to fill up the sandbags the comrades had distributed. Each one of us did what he could.

Every now and then some *fedaiyin* would pass through the camp. They would console us and lift our spirits saying, 'Don't be afraid. There's no danger.' During the last ten days of the month, their visits stopped. And after that none of us dared peep out of the door of the shelter.

They were near us, very near. If any one of us so much as peeped out, we were shot at immediately. They came so near that only a street separated us, with us at the top and them at the bottom. Five people were shot dead, although during our early days as refugees there had been no casualties, except for the time when the bomb landed near the door of the shelter.

One day, a girl was peeping through the door when she saw them sneaking up towards the camp. We never heard a sound. But we knew that the next attack would be on our camp. We knew that the fascists had penetrated the camp next door to George Matta's factory and that they had killed a hundred and twenty people. Seventeen from the Shoqair family died in the other shelter. When the snipers gained control of the main entrance, our people posted guards and dug another door in the back wall. People fled, seeking shelter elsewhere.

At five in the afternoon, we got out with only the clothes on our backs, leaving all our belongings behind. The next day, before the militia had completed its occupation of the area, I went back with a group of people to collect whatever we could carry of the supplies that

had been left behind in the camp. I had to fetch the milk
bottle for my baby brother because my mother's breasts
had dried up and no longer had any milk for nursing him.

After we came out, a lot of people were shot. The
shooting took place as if the people were standing right in
front of the barrel. The sniper would shoot and the people
would fall down one after the other. Lucky the ones who
could escape by the skin of their teeth.

Translated by Sahar Hamouda

Black Lines

Farouk Wadi

Is the sea bleeding, or is it that my heart is weary these days
Ezz al-Din al-Manassra

'It is not my city nor is it yours. Why stay?' she said . . .

The luggage was ready for departure, and the woman was preparing for the voyage. You did not take your eyes off her, but she and the luggage slipped away right before your eyes. Your eyes fell to the cold floor . . . and you remained alone.

Alone . . .

When all the faces disappear in the city night, your face peers into the silence of dreadful loneliness.

Every evening you return to your room. Loneliness inhabits you. You sit without a city and without a woman. Cities leave a borrowed memory to occupy yours. And the woman who was here a few days ago, affirming her presence between the four walls, has become no more than a shadow moving in the cells of memory. You think, you dream, you pull out some old papers . . . letters and poems and projects for stories. You read them for the last time, then shred the papers, shred the words, and envy those who luxuriate in the blessing called a 'homeland', if only because they are able to preserve their intimate papers.

There is no one to keep you company. You wait for a stray voice to burst into your loneliness. You watch a moth hovering around the light. Your eyes follow it as it flutters above your head and then lands on the light, thus casting a wide shadow which fills you with the ecstasy of sensing that some creature shares with you the walls and the loneliness of the city.

She was here, things affirm, as does the echo of her voice: 'This is not my city, nor is it yours.'

She told you about the sun and the sea in her city, and you were together, standing on the shore of the sea by this city, Beirut, as a strange blueness spread over the horizon. The blue was not that which you had believed to be the colour of the sea, just as Beirut was not the city you had believed it to be. So you borrowed a memory from your father and told her about another sea and other cities by a sea your eyes had not seen.

Trying to describe it, she said, 'The sea there has a special smell and its blue is unique.' You failed to find an equivalent statement, for you were incapable of describing it. Her voice then added, 'You will discover that yourself when we meet there.'

Before your eyes, fences, drawn by the absence of a travel document, were erected, and you muttered to yourself, 'We will meet!'

Without carrying a passport, you crossed the borders drawn on the maps. You planted your body in this city, and thus Beirut became a rock. You then recovered the cities locked in the memory and said that the women there will have breasts granting warmth to weary heads.

In the last city, the interrogators said to you, 'You all thought that Amman had become your city as you wandered around her mountains with your weapons ... Amman now belongs only to her people.'

You were silent, affirming your determination to

remain silent before the questions. And Amman too remained silent, after they had washed her face with blood and gunpowder.

And when you carried your graduation certificate and other papers crowded with official stamps, the faces of relatives and friends fixed their questioning glances on you, 'Did you find work?'

You will be allowed no work and you will die of starvation, so they said. You remember the phrase at the foot of the page that has become a companion to all the applications you have submitted for work. 'We do not recommend the appointment of the above-named.'

'No; I found none.'

You will find none. Let's see what your precious graduation certificate can do for you. So they said. So you say I found none, quickly, as if you are trying to shoo away an old fly that has landed on your face. You struggle to slip away for fear of the subject being further discussed.

And at home two old faces greet you, 'Did you find any work?'

You stand broken and keep your answer short, 'We do not recommend the appointment of the above-named.'

You know for certain, 'Amman is not your city. Why stay?' Then you cross the cities towards Beirut without a travel document.

'Did you find a woman?'

Genial in spite of the sharpness of his features, the dark rural face that used always to ask you that question, did not give you enough time to reply. One day, towards the end of September, the distant prison in al-Jafr desert took him away . . .

'I found her, my distant friend, but she is now vanishing behind those crooked black lines on the maps. She had a warm heart and a warm body, but she was a woman with an inclination to travel.'

One, two, three . . .

You measure the distance between you and her according to your inability to travel, and you discover how arduous and difficult it is for you to cross that distance.

All things near become distant, and you feel that the distant woman has become even more distant.

One, two, three ...

Steps are limited, and the way to you, my lady, is far. They said to the prince, you must cross the forest of ghouls to get to the princess ... but did the ghouls ask for a passport?

One, two, three ...

The steps are unwieldy except when you head for your home which is not your home, erasing the traces of your day with weary feet.

Night time ...

And you are without a document proving your identity. That is how you are in this city and all cities, under the threat of deportation at any moment. A moment beyond expectation in which a tired policeman, filled with boredom, standing at the corner of peripheral streets, stares at your face and perceives something which he does not understand. And because he does not understand the things in your face as they are, and because he is filled with boredom, he requests your identity documents.

'Any document to prove your identity.'

Here are the eyes, and that same face upon which boredom is hardened. The same eyes and the same face that, at every moment, you dread encountering.

He shakes you as you stand dumbfounded, 'Your identification?'

You look in your pocket and feign forgetfulness.

'I forgot it.'

He laughs, and thus the boredom slips from his face as he pulls you by the shoulders, and makes you stand in front of another man who has succumbed to slumber, as he delivers his questions, 'Place of permanent residence?'

'None.'

'Work?'

'None.'

And no travel document ... and no woman ... and no sea and no shore.

Alone.

You stand between the walls of a room which they have firmly sealed. You wait for a lost voice that would run towards you, or a moth of the kind that hovers around the light.

The desire for travel awakens within you.

My love . . . Here I come to you, a flock of seagulls thirsting for travel.

One step, two steps, three . . .

You resolve to take the fourth step but bump into the hard cell wall in front of you, and you feel that all the walls are leaning into an embrace ... Ah ... How arduous and difficult it is for you to cross a distance no greater than a single step ... Just one more step.

You see deserts, and many seas crouching in every step, and so many nights separating each step from the next. And when you try to think of how many steps lie stored in the thousands of miles, you are filled with terror.

'Between one step and the next are vast distances that vision cannot encompass.'

You thought.

And the rift between you and the absent woman continued to widen. So you fell on the floor, weary and sad.

The flock of travelling seagulls, at that moment, was taking flight from your body to cross the crooked black lines on the maps.

Translated by Nur Elmessiri

Pizza in Memory of Mariam

Rashad Abu Shawer

The nurse is dark ... no, fair with black, no ... brown eyes.
There are many patients and I'm exhausted. Every now
and then I send her an admiring glance. Perhaps then
she'll let me in to see the doctor. But she looks at the
notebook in front of her and calls out names according to
her list. I try to send her some of my mysterious, admiring,
imploring glances, but she answers the phone and attends
to other things, avoiding the patients and their eyes.

She called me when the bell rang inside just as a patient
was leaving. So I went in. The doctor is grey-haired; his
hair is parted on the right. His features remind me of a
mixture of actors, Jeff Chandler and Robert Taylor. I
would like to have been an actor. I said this to my friend
Khairy a few days ago and he laughed.

I handed the doctor the report I had brought with me
from Romania. He pushed my hand away, smiling confidently as his eyes flew over the report.

'This report comes from Romania,' I told him. 'I was
treated there a couple of months ago. One of my friends
led me ... I mean one of my friends ... he had been treated
by you ... advised me to come here.'

He gestured to me to lie down on a sturdy white bed and
uncover my stomach, which I did. As his fingers pressed
on the edges of my stomach and on my belly near the
bladder, he said, 'Your case is a familiar one: chronic

infections and convulsions. The nerves of the colon are almost frayed away.'

Then he asked me, 'What do you do?'

'I'm hardly working ... I used to ... I write ... I scarcely sleep ... I think of ... Previously, I had been ... Actually, I'm always at the office.'

But this isn't work ...

'You're exhausted,' he said, adding, 'very exhausted. You need a long rest. Your face is a familiar one. You're a young man; why are you so tense? What exactly do you want to do with yourself?'

His fingers pressed, hurting me. I said, 'I used to dream of liberating Palestine, alone even, and then ...'

'You discovered that you're not able to liberate yourself.'

'More or less.'

'You all smoke a lot,' he said. 'You drink a lot, you stay up late, you torture yourselves a lot and then you come to the doctor when it is too late. I'll prescribe a simple tranquillizer for you.'

I sat facing him. He looked me in the eye and said, 'Come back in two months, I can tell you now that you won't be completely cured, but your condition will improve. That's about all I can do.'

I shook hands with him and left. I paid the nurse a hundred Lebanese liras. She asked me if I wanted to take a receipt for the money. I turned around and walked away wishing that I could take her. As I walked down the steps, I laughed at the idea and at the doctor who looked like Jeff Chandler and Robert Taylor, and who didn't care about the report which Professor Ionesco had written for me. Professor Ionesco had explained to me that he despises Eugène Ionesco, the Romanian dramatist, who criticizes his own country, lives in Paris, writes trivial absurdist plays and sympathizes with Zionism.

I stood at the entrance of the building waiting for the rain to stop, watching the students of the American

University. The girls were pretty, with long hair, and they tossed their heads elegantly and coquettishly. Some had their hair cut like boys. Both boy and girl students spoke cheerfully and quickly before they disappeared inside the university entrance, before they walked through the narrow door.

The rain thinned. A light spray, the smell of trees and sea, the sound of explosions and bullets far away. Cold wind striking my face while I walk along the deserted railway tracks, my hand pressing on the prescription in my pocket. Why don't you, almighty doctor, no, not almighty doctor, why don't you, instead of prescribing tranquillizers for me, write, 'He is to be given Mariam, a small house and the child which, when in her womb, was pierced by bullets'?

Mariam, Mariam . . .

Here I am, facing the sea in the rain. The waves are high, the salty spray enters my nose, my throat, even the pores of my body. It fills my soul. I am a lonely man. And you, the worms and the dampness of the grave have left nothing of you or of the baby. Its soft bones decayed and were annihilated. You opened your eyes wide, turned slightly, released a small, sharp cry of pain, and then fell. Your eyes remained open with me inside them and the fear of death and an image of the girl you had wished for (you wanted a girl, and I wanted a boy, and we used to dream and laugh). September came and you left and will not return. I want you, my young wife. The medicine doesn't bring you back, nor does it bring back the laughter (of the girl/boy from the worms' guts and the dampness of the grave).

Roar, you sea, and rise, you waves, high and full of salt! Come out, fishes, you sharks with terrifying jaws, jump from the depths of the sea, out of the bellies of the mighty steel tanks, devour our flesh and dreams and our children, devour the umbilical cords that nourish their tender bodies and soft bones. And you, Mariam, why were you evacuated from the shelter? Why? Didn't you know that they were approaching with the fire of their machine guns and that I am a man who loves you, who wants a boy/girl, whichever, it doesn't matter which, it is you who matters. But you walked out of the shelter and they were frightened or hysterical, advancing, evil, mad . . . firing their guns.

The day we got married, my friend Mohammed fired his gun.* Mother and the women ululated for joy and I said, 'Don't, it's not right. Our neighbour's son died in battle just a few days ago. I don't want singing or ululations, I beg you, Mohammed, my friend, please don't shoot in the air.' Our neighbour's son died a martyr's death and it was I who made him a member of the organization. His father and mother are mourning him. His corpse remained there, on the high rocks in the Golan Heights. Mother of my wife, dearer to me than my own mother, I challenged your scowling oldest son, the mean one, who was against my marriage to Mariam, your son, the merchant, owner of the big shop in Amman, who said, 'He's a *fedai* and he is destined to die. He's also old, and my sister's young . . .' Please tell the girls not to ululate. The small room embraced us, Mariam. I had told you that we'd live alone, just you and I. Your brother, the one in Kuwait, friend from my schooldays, sent us money and wrote, 'I'm on your side. Don't feel embarrassed by my merchant brother's attitude. I myself, my mother and all the family blessed and still bless this marriage.'

Come, waves, rise high, loud, insane! Rise higher, take over and sweep away. Here's the medicine which the very famous, the not almighty doctor, whose fees are only one hundred liras, gave me. Take the Vesalium and the Mycidine; take also the Valium. (Give him Mariam and a

---

*Firing in the air and ululations are traditionally used to express rejoicing, as, for example, at weddings.

small girl with braids; he is to be given Mariam and a boy with long dark hair, black eyes and a little girl with an enchanting smile, a little Mariam with a tiny green uniform . . . Oh Mariam, Mariam, my Mariam.

The cars speed by. Some cars pass by slowly, lovers and lonely men inside them, splashing me with the water which flies up from underneath the wheels while I walk. I follow the ascending asphalt road; up I climb. A face looks down through the clouds. I ask: Almighty God, God of all peoples, you who look down upon us, exactly why did you take Mariam and the still unformed Palestinian creature? Why have you burdened me with seven years of suffering, making me pay all my income to doctors, making me an addict of arak, whisky and Valium, making me stay up late, making me remember – why?

And you, head waiter, at this small, fancy restaurant, bring me a litre of patriotic wine, two pizzas, one without salted sardines (What do you call them? Forgive me, I don't like unpatriotic names) and one with salted sardines; Mariam, while pregnant, craved sardines. Her mother said, 'You're like me, my daughter.' And I said, 'If you go on devouring salted sardines, you'll deliver an unsalted Palestinian sardine. It will fly off to the sea of Palestine to become salty, play and grow in the sea. Then your mother said, 'You're like me in everything, my daughter. I saw your father by the village wells and wished to have him for myself, so God gave him to me. The doors of the sky were open. And you wished for your husband and God gave him to you; the doors of the sky were open . . .'

'But where's the person with you, mister?'

'I've been waiting for this person for years, waiter!'

The waiter (or maybe he was the head waiter) laughed and said, 'Not in our restaurant. This is your first time here.'

The person left. I've been waiting for seven years, ten years, since my mother gave birth to me, since first I saw her in her green uniform and wrote to a schoolfriend who works in Saudi Arabia, 'I want to marry Mariam.' Mariam came and left so quickly, and I'm waiting for her.

'Waiter! Bring me a different wine, a patriotic wine, high in alcohol. The doctor, his medicine and his advice can all go to hell. Keep his worthless degrees and bits of information.

'Waiter, are you doctor or waiter? What is to you if I drink without eating? I'm free and I shall remain free until an aimless or an intended bullet hits me in Beirut or in the South and pierces me and takes me to her who waits there in her grave near the camp in Amman.'

After two litres of wine, both unpatriotic and patriotic, and a pack of strong cigarettes, come, let's see the bill. Here I am, alone, my breast to the wind and the sparrow in my ear and the voice of the waiter, 'But, mister, you didn't eat.' Winking, 'Is she late? She won't come? But if you know that – forgive my intrusion – why are you still waiting for her? The world is full of women who long for a young man like you.'

The stinging, biting wind slaps my face and pierces my skin. I feel dizzy and my body shivers. Between me and the fruit shop it's quite a way; between me and the sea are the local shops. (Those Lebanese! If the Third World War broke out and the world was destroyed, some of them would get to the moon, open shops or put up stalls there and import customers from the planets. They would plant groves, produce good arak and sing, 'O Abu Zuluf, O Molia. Palestine is the root of suffering and the South is in my heart.'* If only they knew how much I love them and how ashamed I am of how obnoxious some of our groups can be.)

'Right here, driver. Thank you.'

The driver says, 'It seems like you've overdone things.'

---

*A line from a typical *mawal*, (folk song) of the Levant. Abu Zuluf is a man's name and Molia is a woman's.

'Yes, but then life has overdone things a millionfold.'

I'm trying to walk straight, not to appear drunk. Abu Hamid will look me in the eye, reproachful and sad, ancient Abu Hamid who, a long time ago, carried the gun and climbed the mountain, who saw Sheikh Ezz Eddin in al-Istiqlal Mosque and heard him speak about *jihad* and the Homeland, who declared as unbelievers those who sell the soil of their grandfathers, who do not struggle against the people who fight against them, whose aim is to drive them out of their homes. Abu Hamid, how old are you? (I was born a long time ago, I don't know when, and I don't know when I'll die. I was injured dozens of times and stayed alive. He who dares, lives long. I neither smoke nor drink; I neither pray nor fast nor disbelieve.) He doesn't hate; he only loves, or despises; he's above all of that. He comes and goes. He goes to the South, visits the young men, and returns. He says, 'I don't guard just anyone; I guard the revolution. I don't open the door for anyone and I don't run after anybody. I love my country. I race to it. I shall live. Don't drink too much. Here you are, back again at the poison . . . There he is, lighting the fire, the young men surrounding him while he tells them the most beautiful stories – and I arrive staggering. My stomach is full of the bitter acidic liquid, but empty of food.

He grabbed me playfully and whispered into my ear, 'You went back to drinking.' He said it reproachfully . . .

I broke down in tears and asked him, 'Didn't Mariam come with a little girl with two braids?'

'She did,' he said. 'She asked for you and when she didn't find you she left.'

'And why didn't she wait?'

'She wants you to wait for her and become the man she knew.'

'She said so.'

'Where, oh, where have you been? The young men in the South, your friends, have been asking after you. They asked whether Beirut has changed you. Why don't you visit them any more, eh?'

I went up to the fire, staggered, held out my hand, warmed up a bit, staggered, and almost fell into the flames. One of the young men held me. Abu Hamid took his *argul** out of his inside coat pocket. He began to play in the wind and the rain in front of the fire. I pulled myself together, went inside and stood facing the lift.

One of the young men said, 'The lift's out of order. Shall I help you walk up?'

Abu Hamid knew. He turned his head, annoyed. The young man understood that he wished him not to.

I climbed the stairs to the madness of the *argul* tunes. When I reached my room on the seventh floor, I opened the door. I opened the windows and I saw many tanks, machine guns and cannons advancing; I saw Mariam and the small girl with the braids and as I dashed forward the bullets penetrated and pierced my body and the *argul* tunes came out of me and flew, scattering into the grey emptiness.

Translated by Magda Amin

---

*a flute-like instrument

Dead is the Yearning

Salih Abu Isbaa

When the military governor summoned me for interrogation, he asked me question after question. I said, 'Dead is the yearning,' and brust into tears, hysterically sobbing. Silence prevailed and all I could hear was my own incessant weeping.

The military governor was smoking his hand-rolled cigarette without taking his eyes from me. Beside me, the *mukhtar** was murmuring something, though I recall only a few of his words. But I remember that he kept repeating, 'What a shame! Oh, what a shame, Abu Hussein. Dead is the yearning.'

My beloved was a rose; her eyes, the colour of pistachio; her lips, lovely, and her cheeks like apples from the Levant. And so the years passed and my hair turned grey with me living there in that distant part of the Homeland.

How could we have parted? But there it is. I searched for them all: Um Hussein, Hussein, Radwa and Samia. And now, where are they?

Al-Ramla is an old city. The *mujahedeen* carry their old guns, resisting and waiting for God's deliverance and for the Arab armies that advance, gain territory and then retreat. We are engaged in a mighty battle that claims

*the village chief

93

many friends as martyrs. The bullets come at me and tear my thigh and I bleed profusely. Abu Salem props me up and tries to help me. The enemy approaches, the shooting intensifies, and the bleeding continues. 'Abu Salem, save yourself before they get you. Me, I'm done for.'

Dead is the yearning, dead.

'What are you doing here in Ramallah? Out with it! Contacting saboteurs, organizing a subversive cell in Ramallah? Come on, tell me!'

I am startled by his words and yet not startled at all. I let out a long laugh – they have opened the gates and the land is now all one, joining what lies in the hands of the enemy with what does not. I carry with me a few gifts as well as the burden of separation, of grief and of yearning. Now that Hussein has become a full-grown man and Samia is of marrying age, I have bought them some gifts and come to Ramallah to look for them. Some friends told me that I would be able to find their house easily. I go to their house, my heart dancing with joy. Um Hussein will see me. Taken by surprise, she will be riveted to the ground. And then I will take her in my arms and she will weep, weep for joy; tears well up in my eyes as I embrace her and she embraces me and then the children come and I embrace them . . .

I stand in front of the door. Should I knock? No . . . The shock might be too great for Um Hussein and the children. Better have someone warn them of my arrival.

No . . . Here I am, standing in front of the door. I knock twice lightly, then step back. I knock again, watch the door, listen closely but hear nothing.

I knock hard. I hear the sound of feeble, shuffling footsteps. The door opens and an old woman asks, 'Who is it?'

'I'm Abu Hussein.'

'Who?'

'Abu Hussein.'

'What do you want?'

'Where's Um Hussein . . . and Hussein and Samia?'

The woman is welcoming. 'Do come in. This is your home. Have a cup of tea.'

I look around the house in which they live: two tiny rooms, no chairs, no furniture.

'But where are they all, *Hajja*?'

Mournfully, the old woman murmurs, 'They left.'

'How come?' I weep and weep. Dead is the yearning, dead. 'Where did they go?'

The old woman consoles me and tries to calm me. 'Do you know that your son Hussein is studying engineering in Cairo? As for Samia, she works in Kuwait. No one except Um Hussein was left, and so she emigrated, like so many others, to join her children.'

To join them . . . to join them . . . And me, how am I to join them, how?

'Answer me. What brought you from al-Ramlah to Ramallah?'

This military governor knows no other question and I know no answers.

The *mukhtar* intervenes, trying to explain: 'As you know, *Khawaja*, in 1948 some families were divided – a single family might be split in two – half here, the rest there. Surely you know all that. Abu Hussein lived there in your area in al-Ramlah while Um Hussein lived here, with us. His children grew up in his absence. One of his sons died without his father ever seeing him. But now that the land has been joined, people, too, want to rejoin each other. Abu Hussein came over to see his family. It is true that they have emigrated, but he still comes here. We have a saying, *Khawaja*: "To catch a whiff of the beloved's scent."'

The military governor remains unconvinced and moves about, agitated. 'Answer me. What brought you from al-Ramla to Ramallah?'

He asks me what brings me here. But is this land not ours, and have they not opened up the borders for us so that we might pass beyond pain and death and yearning?

What is it that brings me here? The very same question that a police officer asked me, years ago, at the Mandelbaum Gate. 'What brings you here, old man?'

I do not answer him. Tears flow from my eyes and I give vent to my grief, anguish and pain. I shake my head and see the children on one side and their parents on the other. I look for my children and wife. I see them and my heart pounds. I see Um Hussein behind the barriers; our eyes meet. 'This is your father,' she tells my son. The boy looks at me with wonder. 'My father? . . . Father!' And I wonder if there are parents, other than Palestinians, who are separated from their children.

Our eyes meet, and yet we dare not speak. Years pass and my three children grow up. We meet here every year for a few hours. The children grow up and I lose one of them and we meet every year across the yearning, the pain and the hope.

Dead is the yearning.

O Governor of the city, I come to sow the land with yearning. My yearning is like nails dug in my heart, their wounds will not heal. Here, O *Khawaja*, is the scent of my loved ones. And is there anything other than the loved ones' scent that can quench yearning?

'You arouse suspicion. A man like you, in your fifties, you ought to be looking to your own comfort. Your family isn't here, so what is the use of coming here? You arouse suspicion. We will let you off this time, but you are not to return. We can let you off once, not twice.'

What's the use of my coming here? My yearning died the moment I came here and didn't find them. Dead is the yearning. I know that my family is not here, but I come to seek comfort . . . I come to seek comfort.

'Off with you and don't let me see your face again. Leave immediately!'

'Leave immediately or you'll come to harm,' the *mukhtar* says to me.

No, I shake my head.

'What is it that you want to do?' he asks.

I do not answer him. He repeats his question. I do not reply.

'What a shame!' the *mukhtar* murmurs. 'The man has lost his mind and will come to a bad end.'

I move away from him.

He yells at me, 'I advise you to leave immediately and never return. I won't intercede on your behalf again!'

Smiling, I roamed the streets and alleys of the city. The sun set and I returned to the house and knocked on the door. The old woman opened the door. She said that the *mukhtar* had passed by and warned her not to let me in but she did not understand what he was saying since this is my home and it is my right to return to it.

She had barely finished what she was saying when we heard a violent knocking on the door. She opened the door. There was a whole unit of the defence army. As they took me away, I glimpsed the *mukhtar* shaking his head in apology and regret.

I spent the night in the prison of Ramallah and no one interrogated me. The following morning, they took me to the military governor, the usual procedure. They never take their regular prisoners to the military governor.

When he saw me, he said angrily, 'You thought I was just joking, you son of a . . .' and he let out a stream of obscenities.

I did not feel the impact of the blow I received though I staggered and fell on the ground. He put his foot on my face and then kicked me several times. After that I had no consciousness of what happened.

The following evening, the interrogator summoned me and charged me with organizing cells of *fedaiyin*. I laughed and laughed while the interrogator swore at me.

Translated by Hala Halim

A Palestinian

Samira Azzam

He spoke hesitantly, the words scraping his dry throat, 'Give me your card. I'll take a look and then return it.'

His neighbour did not seem to understand. So, reaching out irritably with his hand, he repeated, 'Your card. I mean your identity card.'

In response to the irritably extended hand, the neighbour produced a worn wallet from which he took out his ID and gave it to him. Before he stepped through the doorway holding it, a voice drifted past his ear, saying, 'Where are you going with my ID, you Palestinian?'

If the neighbour had heard the insult muttered in reply, he would surely have snatched back the ID from his fingers. But the Palestinian hurried off with it to his shop where he flopped down at the stained table and opened it. He then put his hand in his pocket and pulled out his own new card. It was a glossy green, its cedar-tree emblem unmarred by creases. It was new – he had only received it two weeks earlier. His photo was on one side and, on each of the three folds, there was the circular seal of the Civil Registry Department of the Ministry of the Interior. The fourth seal was on the reverse of the fourth fold. Four seals, circular and explicit; no shadow of doubt could ever penetrate their circumference. They bore the signature of the Chief as well as the Commissioner. The signatures, mysterious and inaccessible, seemed to intertwine and were quite illegible as befitted the signature of those in high places.

The neighbour's ID was no different except for the faded old picture, the details of name, age, date and place of birth, and the fact that it had been creased and battered by dirty and uncaring fingers, fingers that had shown no consideration for that which comes as a natural right, a right for which its owner did not have to invest effort, worry, doubts or money. A card not born of feelings of anger, bitterness or agony at the fact that he remained without a name, in spite of having opened a shop in the neighbourhood where he lived, and having done business there for ten years in cash, on account and sometimes even in crooked dealings. In this corner of the world where he had established a shop not at all different from other shops, he was no more than 'a Palestinian'. By this title they called and knew him and cursed him if the need arose. Just like the Armenian cobbler he had known in his boyhood who had spent thirty years of his wretched life mending and patching shoes for a neighbourhood where no one had bothered, let alone needed, to find out if his name was Hagop (a common Armenian name) or Sarkis or Vartan. 'The Armenian' was the only name he had; as such he lived, as such he died, isolated by his name from the rest of the people, living and dead. Perhaps this appellation created a complex in him so that he never lost his accent, and his interests never rose above the level of people's feet.

The two IDs lie before him; as he fingers them the details dance before his eyes. A customer walks in and he dismisses him with a wave of his hand, without looking up. The man goes off in a huff not knowing why he has no wish to sell. The newspaper slips to the floor and he picks it up; he is terrified by the red headline above some photographs of members of the gang. What's the use of reading the news for the fifth or hundredth time? He would never understand any more than he did already.

The picture speaks for itself. The thin face more than half swallowed up by the glasses, the bald patch starting just above the glasses, hardly indicate a diabolical mind. And others with him of whom he recognizes only one ... he gives the impression of being anything other than what he really is. It was through him that he had met the other one.

Yes, he had been wearing a blue suit when he barged in and bought a box of matches, paying in francs. He had brought out a pack of cigarettes, taken one and offered him another, which he declined. He had smoked half his cigarette at the doorway, facing the street. He came back inside, hovering as if wanting to drag him into conversation, any conversation. But then he came bluntly to the point. He had heard, and he refused to say from whom, that he wished to become a naturalized Lebanese. If he liked, there was only one way ... and the price, yes, there was a price, two thousand liras. A little more than what people normally paid because the authorities were getting stricter and stricter. Palestinians had been ferreting around in their family trees until there was hardly a tree that didn't have a branch in the Lebanon. And as for those lawyers who had grown rich by specializing in naturalization, genealogy was beginning to let them down.

It was too much ... Some years ago he had balked at paying a quarter of this amount to unearth a grandfather from a good Lebanese village or to resurrect a whole new history of his grandfather Abu Saleh who had been born, as far as he knew, and who had died, also as far as he knew, in al-Rama. He had not quite denied him three times before the crowing of the cock, but rather had asked his permission to make use of a geographical coincidence which would exempt him from the word 'Palestinian', a word which linked him to a breed in whom all signs of individuality had been wiped out. The word is uttered pityingly when he refuses to be an object of pity, or with uncalled-for surliness or threateningly, as when rival shopkeepers spit out their venom, spinning it into rumours, intepreting events according to their whims. The threads around him were flimsy yet dense. A cloud of anxiety made him feel as if he, his shop, his four children and his wife were mere playthings to be trifled with by those interpreters of events. His only guarantee against the unknown of multiple deportation was for him to become naturalized. The incentive would weaken whenever the web of rumours loosened, and his fear would die away in the fabric of everyday life. It would become stronger whenever something occurred to shake up his crumbling existence. When his son graduated from school, for instance, he had not been able to hold down a single job for longer than two weeks. The law was explicit; employment in government agencies and in companies was prohibited to aliens. The boy had no option but to flee to one of those desert lands which unite people as brothers in hardship and which deal out wretchedness equally and regardless of nationality.

The incentive grows stronger, especially when, for one reason or another, he intends to go and visit his family scattered here and there, and is forced to wait for an entire week at the door of the government office concerned in order to procure a travel permit. When his father, who lived with his brother in Amman, died, he sent a telegraph saying, 'Postpone for a week or bury him now.' It was the saddest joke the telegraph official had ever laughed at.

Two thousand? Too much . . .

The middleman furrows his brow and taps the tip of his second cigarette against the box before lighting it. 'You won't get an ID for less. I believe you've tried, haven't you?'

Indeed he had tried. For three years his case had swung to and fro between the excuses of the lawyer who eventually wiped his hands clean of everything except half of the agreed fee he had pocketed in advance.

'But will it work for sure?'

'Payment on delivery and we don't charge anything in advance.'

His features soften into a smile. The man takes his leave, his smooth, slick voice filling the corners of the shop, 'Think it over and I'll pass by in a few days.'

He did not think it over by himself, but rather tried to get his wife to think it over too. Overwhelmed by the amount, she said, 'Two thousand? Is it a minister's ID? Others have managed to get it for 300 or 600, even for free!'

Without much conviction but unwilling to let the chance die in the first round, he retorts, 'Two thousand, because we once thought that 300 was too much. One day we may have to pay 10,000. Do you want your son to spend his life in an inferno where it's fifty in the summer, in a country which knows no winter?'

He had touched her weakest spot. She said, 'Do as you like. Two thousand, two thousand. May God never bless their money. That is, if you can raise that sum.'

'I can raise it if I empty half my shop-window. I will hang that ID up in it so that people will know us by a name.'

It is quite usual that a lie be decisive in its truth. Three or four weeks passed and all was quickly concluded. He did not meet the person (who called himself a professor) more than once. On a piece of paper, he had taken down all the details, the name, the names of wife and children, the places and dates of birth. He said he would handle everything – the certificates and the documents. All he needed were the photos and, of course, the two thousand. It wasn't all for him, there were a lot of expenses and even more parties involved.

Yes, more parties involved . . . five photos in the newspaper of five counterfeiters – a gang in the fullest sense of the word. Its leader was a professor and its members were no less professorial than the professor. They had in their possession, according to the paper, a complete set of equipment. One of them had admitted to having counterfeited tens of IDs. Oh, Grandpa Abu Saleh, you've let me down. I bet you didn't want to live two lives – one tending an olive orchard in al-Rama, and the other, setting up a vineyard on a Lebanese mountain slope.

Tear it up, tear up the paper and gouge out this professor's eyes from behind his black glasses. What good will it do you to tear up the paper? In so doing, you would not be erasing the reality of the lie, or cancelling out the fact of your having paid two thousand for a piece of paper and of your having co-operated with forgers, and of . . . Why hadn't he realized this before? He felt the flames consuming him all at once. Could they possibly have revealed the names of their clients? How stupid of him . . . Could there be any doubt that this was the eventual conclusion? How else would the authorities be able to recover the forged IDs?

Dupe or accomplice? Having paid two thousand which had devoured half his shop-window, he is a dupe. By the time the facts have been recorded in the police statements, he will be wasted to the bone, his foolishness fuel for his neighbours' cigarette smoke.

Tear it up. Tear it up for it has begun to eat up your flesh. Why did you put it back in your inside pocket? It is not, for all its two thousand, any more valuable than the newspaper which costs you a quarter of a lira. Tear it up – your empty shop-window will be full one day and your own identity will remain void until you can fill it with something other than forgery, other than the deceit of forgers.

Tear it up. Or do you need more proof? Newspapers sometimes trade in lies but they do not dress up their lies with five pictures of persons of whom you knew two. You'll have the honour of the others' acquaintance when you're confronted with them.

Are you afraid of tearing it up even as you hold it between your thumb and forefinger? Tear it up, tear it up for it's worth no more than the paper on which it is printed. But, no. Keep it in your inside pocket. Keep it, for your tearing it up won't conceal or cancel anything.

He sits down and gets up. Then sits down and gets up again. Facing the street, he stumbles around the shop like a blind ox. He can stifle his anxiety under the façade of everyday life, peaceful in its monotony, resigned to its fate, dreaming of nothing. The gas station pours its fuel into the bellies of shiny cars, the fruit dealer wipes the orchard dust off the apples, diligently trying to make them red, the butcher hacks away at his hanging meat and the barber massages a passive head that does not sweat anxiety like his.

He comes back from the door, looking at the torn newspaper. He bends over it, picks up the pieces, screws them into a ball and throws it away. Once again, he turns to face the street. He sees the eternal basket. It is suspended in front of him by a rope from the second floor just over his shop. It is swaying carelessly underneath the balcony. The neighbour's voice wafts down requesting something or other. She always wants something . . . and remembers only in instalments . . . But this time, he does not hear her. Let her shout as she pleases. He won't sell to anyone. But the voice doesn't give up and neither does the basket. The woman's careless voice extends like a bridge over the street, reaches the apprentice in the mechanic's shop opposite and says in a carefree drawling accent: 'Hey, boy! Tell the Palestinian to put a bottle of Cola for me in the basket.'

Standing unsteadily behind the counter, the Palestinian could feel the drawling voice penetrating through his jacket to his inside pocket. It tore the ID up into tiny fragments which rustle in his pocket, quietly.

Translated by Karaz Mona Hamdy

The Trellised Vine

Liana Badr

The storm took me by surprise.

The raindrops colliding with the windscreen made a trickling sound, raindrops as big as goose eggs and just as oval, solid and white. Splattered in their cruel collision with the things of the world. The clusters of greenery suspended from the branches of the trees became a pond of waves. The sky was a dust-coloured tattoo. The ground, mixed with thunder, turned into a rehearsal for a nature so violent it resembled doomsday.

The roof of the round gymnasium, when I got there, assumed an undiluted splendour in the shadow of the rain. It seemed like a celestial dome, repelling flying sparks brought on by the storm. I strode towards the door enthusiastically. Beneath my clothes I had stuffed a book of paintings I meant to present to one of the trainees who usually brought her little son along to our workouts. I would look at her, amused by his mischief and his clinging to his mother. In her turquoise training suit, with her flowing honey-toned hair and baby face, she reminded me of the paintings of the artist whose book was in my hand.

I pushed the door of the gymnasium open to find her changing her clothes. She was taking off her clothes to put on her training suit. I quickened towards her. It seems my quiet, hasty approach confused her. It would have been hard for her to understand my Palestinian accent, nor was I fluent in French – which she spoke. Before, I had not dared use my voice to ask her nationality. Most of the trainees who spoke French were Arab women. My enthusiastic entry and hasty steps had startled her. The child was not at her side as usual. So shocked was I by her sullenness that I tossed the book towards her. I could not bring myself to explain. She caught the book in her hands as though it were a stone thrown from a distant, unknown place. I turned around and left.

Those soft goose eggs keep hitting against the metal roof of the gymnasium, cymbals sounding and crazed lightning glimmering. I force myself to control my limbs and concentrate on following the trainer's instructions. The terrible crashing in the sky is accompanied by an infernal thunder. It takes me back to Beirut. Everyday the shelling, every single day. Nor is any one sound ever repeated twice. Blasts, explosions, rumbles, earthquakes, each with a different resonance. My blood boiled. I trembled all over. This is no shelling. Yet, it is the very same sound. The weight of the movements bows me down and the sound becomes louder. My body bends like an aluminium tube sending back electrified sound waves. The teacher keeps glancing towards me, noting the burden that locks my ribs motionless. She keeps at me with her instructions. I cannot reveal to anyone here what's upsettting me, because I cannot speak like them. Their words go through me, words that ooze between their fingers, pass beside me, but with an echo that returns to me before they become mute again. Fear reshapes my body into metal plates. My sluggish movements are as ineffectual as the instructions of the teacher. I try. The world roars around me. Waves of compressed air roll in succession with a host of downpours and thunderbolts. I force myself to move but my eyes remain fastened on the metal ceiling that looks like a huge metal plate hanging upside down above us. Will it soar, take off, leaving us at the very heart of the storm? Will it turn into an inflatable tent, flying like a balloon in space? Everything is possible. Roofs do fly off like balloons blown aloft by mad winds.

Tents! Ceilings. Tents!

But it stopped, at last, the rain.

Home.

I'm afraid of crossing the doorstep to go inside. A flood of water surrounds the gate. The ground is streaked with water channels. The walls drip and the windows are saturated while the wood is bloated. Humidity settles like giant drones clutching on to the air that is saturated with static electricity. I wonder a while about what to do, seeing that I cannot bring myself to go in and stay put within four walls; I fight off a sense of suffocation between cement walls.

I've found it!

I'll go to that trellised vine and pluck some of its leaves. How often have I directed my gaze at it, unable to stretch out my hand. I did try once, only to find curious eyes full of hate focused on me. I felt embarrassed and withdrew. My memory was still swarming with the stories about the strange things that had befallen the Palestinians when they returned here after Beirut. Many a time were their motives viewed with suspicion. They were stalked by the field and orchard watchdogs, prey to their fangs whenever their hands reached out to the vines, the leaves of which others never bothered to pick.

Today is the day, the day of carrying out the plan to conquer the trellised vine and pick its leaves. In the wake of this deluge of rain, no one will be disturbed by this strange act.

On my way to the vine, I cross the quinine trees with their massive roots and wooden seeds piled up on the curb like so many dainty thimbles. The tall palm trees evoke in my imagination a mysterious nostalgia for Jericho. Creepers, elms and mulberry trees, all these were planted by the colonialists and left to embellish the streets after they returned to their homelands. I cross an ancient botanical paradise designed by the European imagination to fit the size of their dreams or their fantasies of what Africa should be all about.

The vine! I took the straw basket and approached it. The leaves are drenched, immersed in the dusk light reflected in them. The branch leaning towards the street had, with the force of that gust of rain, dropped even closer to the asphalt. The vine chaotically crept up to the first-floor windows of the building nearby. It did not belong to anyone; it was clear it had sprouted in that particular spot by mere chance. A cared-for vine is unmistakable. Its tentacles would be entwined with a captivating elegance around branches hidden between the leaves, its grapes, silver-green clusters. Supplied from the abundance of its leaves, we would prepare the stuffed vine leaves which in our homeland is a major festive event. It is an unquestionable testimony to the start of spring, of its quiet creeping entry into the dark corners of kitchens, and replaces the few heavy vegetables that are our winter fare.

Yesterday, the visitor from Acre pronounced the word 'homeland'; she could not understand. 'What is it you are saying? I thought you meant Lebanon.' He poked fun at her and reproached her for confusing things. 'Is this possible? Is this how you hear things?' He laughed at her. Slowly he repeated the word 'homeland', spelling it out letter by letter. Then he accused her of forgetting. How could she have lost her sense of what words stood for in that era of the North? The North of Africa, the North of Lebanon, the North of anywhere, or the left of it – Lebanon or elsewhere. Had she really lost her sense of words and of meaning in the era of the North, as he said?

Yet, in the wake of this heavy downpour, she had decided to make a dish from the aroma of the Homeland, the very soil of the homeland with its unseen clusters of grapes. And what of it? Even homesickness can take on this crude expression.

She stretched out her hand and arranged the glistening leaves in batches at the bottom of the basket. The few passers-by on their rushed way to the bus-stops eyed her idly and with curiosity. Their clothes and light overcoats were drenched. The soles of their shoes were disjointed from so much wading through the streams which still flowed though the rain had stopped. She ignored their curious glances and pounced on the leaves, gathering them with her red painted nails. She sank her nails into the flesh of the strings bearing the glistening leaves. There, meaning the homeland, the process of leaf picking had its special rules and rituals. The women of the neighbourhood would gather around the woman who was on the ladder and each would get her share of the leaves. That piquant, appetizing aroma of vine leaves stuffed with rice and minced meat would penetrate each home and leave its imprint on all the doorways.

With the picking of each leaf, the vine leaned down, moving slowly, leaning down. The storm had washed away that heavy layer of smog from car exhaust and smoke of chemical factories under which the vine had bent. It was as though the vine was now revealing a secret complicity with she who cared for it. It glistened breathtakingly in the breeze of the departed rain. With a languorous pleasure, she moved her hands over its tender shoots.

Suddenly, a man stepped before her, right out of the emptiness and stillness of the square. She recovered her composure when she noticed his navy blue suit with the yellowish copper buttons. He was one of the guards of the ruling party's headquarters, which were on one of the floors of the building.

'What are you doing?'

' . . . '

'You're Palestinian! . . . Is this for a dish? . . . How?'

It seemed as if the precondition for reconciliation depended on her giving him a description of the recipe.

She produced all the expressions necessary to describe the process. She stretched out her palm. Opening it, she made the gesture of spreading the leaf on the palm, coarse side up, so that the outside would be the smooth side. Then you go like this: she bunched up the fingers of her right hand, re-enacting for him the motion of rolling the leaf around the small lump of rice. Here we go! This is it. The man was taken by the charm of the description. A woman with a face radiant with suppressed laughter as she describes to him the strange recipe, and a vine glistening around her in the aftermath of rain.

'I forgive you,' the guard said, 'I won't report you for trespassing in front of party headquarters. But, on the sole condition that you let me have a taste of the dish.'

On her way home, she was overcome by a deep confusion. What the man said made sense. He is entitled to a taste of the strange dish. This is our custom in the homeland. It is unthinkable that a family should prepare the dish of the new season without sending some plates of it to the neighbours. Yet, the guard, how? Who would dare take a dish to the headquarters? He is no neighbour, not even an ordinary man. He was someone whose task was to safeguard the place against the likes of her.

On the way back, torrents of water flowed – gathering at the foot of the incline by the roundabout leading to her house. A metal dome loomed up in the midst of the water. The boys and students were pointing at it agitatedly and loudly. It was a sunken car whose surface glimmered like the silvery green scales covering a huge brown dragon's body. A metal dragon vanquished by the storm, clothed with bits of dry leaves, logs of wood and floating refuse, a reservoir for remnants of garbage and fruit peel.

Drowning is a bad omen. It's a sign that I should not return.

I turned and went back home without looking behind me.

Translated by Hala Halim

And They Confiscated Joy in My City

Mohamed Ali Taha

One day his donkey said, 'O Sheikh, I'm tired of wandering about. Have mercy on me! May you rest in heaven peacefully.'

Sheikh Nasr al-Din* took pity on his donkey and parted from him with burning tears.

A few days later the sheikh became bored with his stay and borrowed his neighbour's horse. Mounting the horse, he said, 'You are a good horse, and the son of good horses. I have left the reins loose, so choose any spot on this earth to make a diverting and delightful trip, for as you see the worries of our age are many.'

The horse drank from the water of the Mekong River and gave a long sharp neigh. The sheikh gazed at the plains and forests and smiled, while the horse raced against the wind, tirelessly crossing the wilderness until he reached the gate of Bab al-Amoud in the sacred city. A crowd gathered and a girl came forward offering him a plate full of smiling wounds. He took it and said, 'The self-same image. And Sheikh Nasr al-Din has certainly seen plenty.' He made a movement with his hands as if taking some ointment to bekohl the wounds. Laughter,

---

*Also referred to in Arab folk tales as Joha. He is well known both for his wit and his wisdom.

ululations and popular songs rang out. The February clouds dispersed, allowing the sun's warm golden rays to dance on the stones of the walls, playfully sneaking through the lanes, tempting the young to run and play and the old to bathe.

A police car, bearing some resemblance to Solomon's ring and the star of David, came and fired numerous shots.

Through a loudspeaker, its driver said, 'Gatherings are strictly forbidden. The police will shoot anyone who violates the order. Anyone shutting up their shop shall have it confiscated. Shouting is not allowed. Singing is forbidden, except by special permission!'

Threats mingled with the singing of the crowd . . . and bullets followed speech. The soldiers' batons were unleashed on the heads and backs of men, women and children. The visiting sheikh's horse whinnied and neighed after the streets had emptied of people and nothing remained except broken pieces of wood, stones, a headscarf and a *falafel* sandwich from which only one or two bites had been taken . . . and a boy's toy and a schoolgirl's bag.

The sheikh was confused, but said, 'You, too, Nasr al-Din?'

He loosened the horse's reins and headed down towards the gate. Upon entering the gate, tears flowed from the horse, wetting his whiskers. He pulled on the reins and said, 'Since the days of Tamerlane to the age of President Ford, your donkey, Nasr al-Din, has not shed a tear. He has wandered much and had seen much, but his eyes have never known tears . . . So how come, the son of good ones, the friend of Salah al-Din . . . his whiskers are wet, his eyes red and his nose damp?! Patience my friend . . . or else . . . by Allah I'll call him.'

So the horse held his head up, feigning pride, and walked on until he met an old man who had lost his walking stick.

The sheikh said, 'Tell me . . . haven't they learned yet? . . . why did they do this?'

The old man threw the sheikh a sad, sarcastic look and then continued stumbling about. So the sheikh said to the horse, 'By Allah, if my donkey were here, he would've known the old man ... for we've met him many a time in many a place!' The horse continued to walk, sparks flying as his hooves struck against the market tiles.

'Stop, damn you.'

A shot rang out. The horse neighed and whinnied and the soldiers, as quick as lightning, pounced on him. They tied the sheikh's hands and blindfolded him with a black rag, whereupon he said, 'Since your car came to the gate of Bab al-Amoud the children have been screaming. It's become overcast.'

They dragged him to the Maskoubiyya Prison and the horse was left to wander in the city lanes, asking for a knight, until he reached the courtyard of al-Asqa Mosque.

At the police station they asked for his name.

'Joha.'

'Your father's?'

'My mother's name is Fatma.'

'Address?'

'Around the stoves in homes ... in cafés ... and simple workshops ... and ... I won't say more.'

'Profession?'

'To sow smiles on people's faces and plant happiness in their hearts.'

'Joha, you are accused of desecrating our city and of inciting the people to anarchy. And we are civilized people.'

'I know, I know.'

'You are also accused of entering forbidden areas. You are a danger to society.'

'His eyes are full of wood and yet he asks about the straw in my eyes!'

'Take him away.'

'What about my horse, Field-Marshal-General-Aluf-Pasha?'*

They led him to a dark room and the jailer closed the door firmly. The sheikh moved his feet around to get a feel of the ground beneath him . . . one step . . . two . . . three, and his foot stumbled over a body. He shivered and cried out, 'In the name of Allah . . . Who's there?'

'You?!' came the reply. 'Welcome, Sheikh Nasr al-Din.'

'You know me?'

'We've welcomed you twice in the light of day. The first at the gate of Bab al-Amoud and the second at our aunt's house.'

'May Allah neither have mercy on your aunt nor bless her house.'

Laughter rang out. The jailer opened the door and cursed their mothers' private parts. They answered him in kind, making his whole body shake with anger, so he threatened them with this, that and the other.

'So when,' the sheikh asked him, 'are these bogeymen coming . . . Are you going to let them out of their bottles when they've been put there by Solomon?'

The jailer slammed the door angrily, so the sheikh cried out to him, 'Go easy on your nerves, son . . . you still have a few days of work before you.'

For a time all was silence . . . till the sheikh broke it, saying, 'I just don't understand. Why has all hell broken loose?'

'Joy is forbidden in our city,' replied the first prisoner.

'The smile is outlawed,' said the second prisoner.

'Feast days are confiscated,' said the third.

'Growing flowers,' the fourth prisoner, lying on his back, added, 'is an act of sabotage.'

'By Allah,' said the sheikh, 'how have you reached such a state?'

*_Aluf_ is Hebrew for 'general'

'We can take all this but not the hot morning bath.'

'Followed by a cold one.'

'Then comes preparing the bride.'

'Followed by burning between the thighs.'

'Stop! Stop!' screamed the sheikh. 'Stop lest I weep.'

'When you weep, you fall.'

'And when you fall, you fall to signing.'

'And when you sign, you become a rag on a rubbish heap.'

'And when you become a rag, you appear on all channels of the media.'

'Not since the one-legged goose was presented to Tamerlane,' the sheikh commented, 'have I heard the likes of what you say.'

'If you were to present it today, the goose would have one eye.'

'And one ear.'

'And no heart...'

And they all laughed. But the sheikh did not laugh.

'Are you crying?'

'No.'

'What are you thinking?'

'By the true promise of Allah for the oppressed. By Bilal and Amar and the dark woman.'*

'Ha, ha and Abu Gahl and Abu Sufian and Omayya Ibn Khalaf and al-Walid Ibn al-Mughira.'*

'The story repeats itself over the ages, so don't be sad.'

'And do you know history, O Sheikh?'

'Only those who make it really know history. Just as woman is only known by man, and the land by the peasant.'

'But...'

---

*Bilal, Amar and the dark woman were Muslim heroes of a very humble origin at the time of the Prophet Mohamed, whereas Abu Gahl, Abu Sufian, Omayya Ibn Khalaf and al-Walid Ibn al-Mughira are members of the aristocracy who opposed Islam.

'What, my sons?'

'If the chief of the western alley marries a sweet dark-skinned girl from the eastern alley against the wishes of her family and against her own will ... what will happen?'

'Ha, ha ... a marriage of mules ... they'll only beget little kicks.'

Translated by Randa Elgeyoushi

The Homeland

Mahmoud Shuqair

1

I was contemplating the city wall when the soldier shouted, taking me unawares, 'Hey! Stop! What are you doing here?'

'This is my city and I am contemplating its wall,' I replied.

'This, your city? Rubbish!'

He pushed me savagely ahead of him; I walked on for a distance. I then turned on him, pulled a knife from my pocket and plunged it into his neck. The blood gushed out of his body and flowed on to the pavement. I ran off. The tanks and army patrols pursued and cornered me. Not knowing what to do, I looked all around me. Then, beating my wings, I flew up into the sky. I thought that I was safe, but they had spread out nets and traps. They cornered then arrested me and, after plucking my feathers, they put me in a cage. They threw me into prison with common criminals.

2

The prisoners said, 'What did you do, boy, for them to bring you here?'

'I was contemplating the wall of my city,' I said, 'and they didn't like it.'

'You're lying,' they said, 'but, never mind. Since you've

come from beyond these hateful walls, come on, tell us an amusing story.'

I cleared my throat and said, 'Gentlemen, once upon a time there was a sultan who inflicted suffering on his people.'

'Leave politics aside, boy,' they bellowed. 'It's a subject we've become bored with.'

'All right, here's another story. One day, hunger passed through the city and decided to dwell in it.'

'This is a story we know. We don't want to speak about hunger; it is with us day and night.'

'I'll tell you the story of the woman who betrayed her husband the merchant, with her lover the stable boy,' I said.

'Yes,' the criminals cheered. 'This is a story we know and which we don't get bored with hearing.'

And I went on telling this story during the long prison nights.

3

My stay in prison was long. One day I was sitting in a narrow yard trying to catch a bit of sunlight, when I remembered my grandfather who had said to me on 5 June: 'Get on the donkey, boy. We're going to the Homeland.'

We mounted the donkey, my grandfather and I, and the people said, 'Look how inconsiderate they are.'

So my grandfather said, 'Get off, boy.'

I got off and my grandfather continued to ride on the donkey alone. So the people said, 'How cruel! He lets the boy walk without taking any pity on him.'

Dismounting from the animal, my grandfather said, 'Get on, boy,' and he continued to walk, exhausted.

The people said, 'There's no respect any more: this is the age of defeat.'

Enraged, my grandfather shouted, 'Get off, boy.'

And the three of us walked side by side, my grandfather,

the donkey and I, while the people watched us, amazed and stunned.

Taking me unawares, the guards shouted, 'What are you doing, boy?'

'I'm recalling the story of my grandfather who died in the war,' I said.

'Liar,' they said. 'You're rewriting old stories, and that shouldn't be done.'

'Come on,' they said. 'Get up.' So I got up.

They plucked my feathers, blindfolded me and shoved me into a cage. They led me down endless roads and at the borders of my violated Homeland, they said, 'This is where you leave from.'

'This is my Homeland,' I said, 'and I refuse to obey your orders.'

'In front of you is a country called Lebanon. If you don't go, we'll kill you.'

They aimed their weapons. I left, turning my back on the borders of my Homeland.

4

I sat on the balcony of the house; my eyes travelled to the peaks of the green mountains. Sadness crept into my heart, so I climbed down the stairs and headed towards the seer.

'Because I've lost my Homeland,' I said, 'I am sad.'

'In such a case,' she said, 'you ought to extinguish your sadness in the bodies of women.'

I gazed at the seer's body but was let down and disgusted by what I saw.

I left the seer and went out into the streets of the city, where I saw a swarm of girls sashaying along.

'By my plundered Homeland,' I said, 'I implore you, O girls of the city, to bring your bodies near mine, for now that I've lost my Homeland, sadness is my garb.'

The city girls laughed at me and said, 'Whoever leaves his Homeland to be plundered by the greedy deprives himself of the pleasure that bodies can bring.'

Grief weighed heavy in my heart and I took my handkerchief out, hoping that the tears would obey me, but to no avail. I lingered in the streets and saw another group of city girls making their way as gracefully as gazelles.

'By my plundered Homeland,' I said, 'I implore you, O city girls, to remember, when you undress in those houses with lowered curtains, a dark young man who lives in the streets.'

The girls swayed and said teasingly, 'Whoever leaves his Homeland to be plundered by the greedy deprives himself of the pleasure of bodies.'

Where, oh, where do I go with all this sadness coming down, drop upon drop, on my body? I squeezed my eyes so that the tears could flow but found nothing but dryness.

Without thinking, I started running through the city streets. Breathless, I stopped in front of a warehouse and suddenly came upon a girl who smiled tenderly at me. I reached out to pluck the pomegranate of her breast. I was bitterly disappointed to discover that the girl was nothing but a wax statue. I looked for a way out for my tears but found none.

I decided to go to the sea, hoping that my eyes might be moved to tears. I found the sea throwing itself at the feet of the city as if it were a peasant broken by fatigue. I complained about my condition to the sea then listened. The sea started to speak in a cold, monotonous tone. Clothing myself in sadness, I left it and hurried to the grave of the martyrs. I thought this an appropriate place for letting the tears flow. The gravestones were telling everything about my Homeland. I saw all the villages and cities: Bissan, Jaffa, Nazareth, Gaza, Jerusalem. I bowed down my head in awe and reached for my heart, hoping that the tears might flow. The stoniness and obstruction terrified me, and I ran back to my room.

5

The Fascists were burning Beirut's body and darkness was

crawling over her in shame. I closed the doors and the windows securely and said, 'Now is the time to withdraw from danger.' Throughout the long night, a sad hymn in which I recognized my mother's voice crept into my ears, 'Taysir is entrusted to you, Almighty God, Taysir is entrusted to you.' Agitated, I got up. I turned on the light and left the house. Bullets were glittering in the sky of the city and bombs were exploding over the houses and across the roads. Abu Zar, a young man from the tribe, was carrying his gun at one of the turnings. Turning to me, he said, 'Why do you look sad, young man?'

'A strange wind has blown over my Homeland,' I said, 'and so it was lost.'

'What did you do?' he asked.

'I took shelter from the wind by putting my head under my wing,' I said.

'Then what happened?'

'I was uprooted by the wind.'

'And now, where are you going? Don't you hear the bullets?'

'My mother is urging me to keep myself safe,' I said, 'and I have to obey her.'

'And where, young man, is your mother?' he said.

'Hostage in my confiscated Homeland.'

'So, to be obedient, you go out into the downpour of bullets?'

'I have come to hate waiting,' I said, 'and my mother's voice keeps me from sleeping.'

The young man looked me over with interest and then said, 'Follow me.'

So I walked behind him from road to road, becoming more confident the further down the road I ventured. The bullets were pouring down like rain and the young man's rifle shook, towering in space.

Translated by Magda Amin

IV
Babel

Fear

Mohamed Tamila

I did not notice that the streets were empty of cars, and the pavements of pedestrians, until I was half-way to the city centre. I looked around in every direction and saw nobody at all. I said, 'Maybe today's a feast day,' but then remembered that there was no curfew on recognized feast days. I said, 'Maybe, for some reason or other, it's forbidden to walk around in the streets. Who knows?' but then remembered that it had not been announced on the radio. I tried to recollect whether any such announcement had been broadcast, only to remember that I had not owned a radio for years. I said, 'So it is a curfew after all. What business is that of mine?'

As I was about to go on with my walk, I saw a man hurrying towards me, screaming, 'Run away . . . run away.' The man passed in front of me without stopping. I watched him until he had disappeared into a side street, still waving his arms about as if his clothes had caught fire. I said, 'He's mad. I have to go on with my walk.'

I walked on. A woman bumped into me from behind. When I turned around to investigate, she yelled into my face, 'Run away, man . . . run away quickly.' Before I could find out what the matter was, she had vanished into an alley. I said, 'She's mad. I have to go on with my walk.'

I walked on. A child crossed the street with a speed that

astonished me. Before he disappeared into an alley, he
yelled, 'Run away, man.'

Without waiting another moment, I flew like the wind,
screaming with all my might, 'Run away, people, run
away, all of you.'

Translated by Sahar Hamouda

A Chapter from the Book of Present Days

Mahmoud al-Rimawi

'. . . As for the summer of AD 1982, the Hebrew state
successfully overran Lebanon, an Arab League member
country and signatory together with its sister countries of
a joint Arab defence pact. The invasion, described by
observers as total violation, led among other things to the
destruction of camps, frustration of the apple season,
paralysis of the Lebanese army, annihilation of a flight of
a rare species of stork and to the breaking out of the warm,
generous Lebanese *mawals*,* in addition to the total siege
of the capital Beirut. Beirut, only a few years before, was
the meeting place of lovers, the playground of artists, a
major centre for concluding business deals, the printing
press of the Arabs and the regional stronghold, dedicated
to the amusement of the rich and influential.

'And so it was, three days after the invasion, Lebanon's
nights became starless, its morning sun screened off
behind dense smoke. This momentous event occupied
public opinion across the globe, in particular the interest
of various channels of the Western media, some of which
discovered, thirty-four years after the establishment of
the Hebrew state, that this country commits Nazi

---

*A *mawal* is a poem in colloquial language, often sung to the accompaniment of a
reed pipe.

atrocities in cold blood. Coverage of these events was up to date, day by day, hour by hour, ranging from the detention of thousands of children and very young men, a lot of whom had been fired at while the rest had been named the RPJ* children, to a militia girl who stood proudly and submissively before an Israeli soldier, giving him flowers of welcome and wishing he would beget on her a son, to an old woman embracing a gun, having long awaited Arab soldiers, to an Israeli Druze leader being proclaimed ruler over the Shouf region, to mothers and youngsters scooping brackish water from the streets to quench their deadly thirst, to rats nibbling at the seats of the cinema where rest the slumberers of Beirut's long nights, to an old man crawling and dragging the remainder of his years from Sidon to Beirut in order to avoid seeing the invading soldiers there, to fat flies buzzing on faces and never leaving them, to a statement issued by a former US President about Begin's insolence in dealing with the US administration although occasionally this insolence was called for, to a Lebanese woman in nightclothes raising her arms in al-Rawsha completely overtaken by panic and terror, beseechingly screaming at the skies to intervene and stop the blind, brutal bombardment, to the statement of a distinguished American intermediary that the Israelis are not joking, to booby-trapped children's toys parachuted by the planes of the Hebrew state into streets, into green fields and on to doorsteps, to soldiers looting all that they could of the furniture from homes in Sidon and Tyre as well as from the offices in Beirut International Airport, to the unmistakable smile of a Palestinian leader following a spate of intense bombardment, thus prompting an American reporter to ask him, "I see you're smiling . . . are you happy?"

'"And why not?" he answered with wet lips.

*a Russian-made gun

'Ranging, too, from UNRWA's attempts to withdraw the food stock from hungry besieged Beirut, to amputation by candlelight in the remaining hospitals, to a US-made devastating bomb called the 'hollow' bomb successfully tried out on a standing building known as al-Sanaa which housed 250 refugees, all killed under the ruins during one of the chapters of the dirty violation which was termed 'a defensive operation' by the US president, to this and so much more. The thick, warm human blood of people, joined together in their real and definite desire for life, flowed – an abundant flow of lively, congested, purple blood equal to the flow of Israeli, American, Arab and international statements. In protest against the silence, men and women, too, flowed, marching in New Delhi, Bonn, Paris, Islamabad, Rome, Washington, Dacca, New York, London, Tel Aviv, Athens and Madrid, loudly condemning the bloody aggression. Except similar protesters did not flow in most of the Arab cities, resplendent then with varieties of enslavement, cement and rabid consumption, in view of the fact that the rulers have gone beyond such fruitless ways, for if three Arab human beings go on a march in public and shout out statements like those expressed by the ruler himself in newspapers, radio and TV, about struggle, revenge, negligence and humiliation, they will vanish in the darkness of the pit. For the word in the mouth of the ruler is different from that in the mouth of the ruled, and the rules of citizenship are the same as the rules of the monkey game (see not, hear not, talk not). If observance of these golden rules in normal circumstances and at times of dull peace is a necessary duty, it is doubly so in times of crises and wars and in times of deciding the destiny of nations. And so one can see that the invasion was, among other things, a profound and dreadful shock to the conscience of ordinary people, who know that animals react instinctively in self-defence when threatened, and who became suspicious about almost everything. They realized that, in fact, up to the time of the aggression, they had been victims of a great and costly deception, whereas our rulers kept their composure and stood steadfast and courageous applying the poet's saying, "Steadfast is my enemy in victory, and steadfast am I in defeat."

'To the common folk, and as the siege of Beirut (which represented for them their own cities and capitals) tightened, the shock turned into something akin to a constant shiver down the spine, a blockage in the arteries of life, accompanied by a state of nervous congestion, psychotic sickness and muted dismay. These people, in the state that they were in, saw with their own eyes some tangible evidence of what an Arab writer had asserted: that an Israeli epoch was threatening to leave its imprint on Arab life, meaning also that it was a period of Israeli-dictated conditions, Israeli-determined policies and crude Israeli strategic intervention in the plight of the region. They did not, however, see anyone pausing before or considering the shower of omens of the dreadful epoch. Although many practical and simple proposals were put forward to confront the unrestrained Israeli monster, one by one they were all spurned for, as the saying goes, "our real strength lies in our weakness". And so Arab and Islamic radio stations never let up on playing such popular songs as "First Love", "Let's Not Part", "Sitting at Home Alone", "We'd Like to Get Married by the Feast" and "My Lover's Shoes are My Size". Song followed song as the shelling increased and the siege tightened with such songs as "Creamy Moon", "Let Me Love", "Your Delicate Figure", "Oh My Lemon", "Why, Oh Why, Neighbour", "The Dark Woman Passed", and "He Fed Me and I Fed Him Dried Plums". Between each song and the next, a thousand shells fell over the heads of the people of hungry, thirsty, besieged Beirut, while the television set transmitted American Westerns, Indian soap operas and intrigues and TV serials on the conflict between the body and the soul, the big question being, 'who will win?' In the meantime, those in charge displayed, for the first time, a deep hesitation and a put-on declination regarding a harmonious get-together summit. One reporter counted nine invitations that did not even elicit a response, thus prompting the wife of an Arab ruler who dabbles in power to admit that it was truly "the age of the great humiliation". Though, to be fair, it must be said that the ninth invitation, which was made seventy days after the aggression, elicited some response, for an Arab minister heralded the good news that a summit may be convened ... a full month from the date thereof, when by that time a thousand more buildings had become ruins on the heads of their inhabitants in Beirut, though, at the time the statement was made, Beirut had not, in all honesty, been totally destroyed.

'It was a horrific and terrible crisis. A crisis that made heads bow in shame, hair turn grey from sheer atrocity, faces pale and bodies shiver, as so aptly and eloquently put by our orators who leave nothing undescribed. But before long, the trial of trials, even if not so short a while, slowly turned, bit by bit, day by day, year by year, and one experience in falling and rising after another ... it slowly turned, by the will of the All Empowering Victor, into a blessed sacred curse afflicting the enemy, and all those of the same mind as the enemy, be they spectators, conspirators or gloaters, as shall be more fully explained in the coming chapters ...'

August 1982

Translated by Randa Elgeyoushi

The Man Who Lies a Lot

Zaki Darwish

'But you do remember the first time?' I said.

'I'll try to remember,' he replied. 'It was such a long time ago ... When? ... When? ... I think it all goes back to school-days. What happened before that, I can't remember – maybe it was all a dream ... Do you know children take their dreams for reality?'

This matter is of great importance, for the boundaries between one and the other are sometimes illusory ... It all goes back to the first lie ...

We (Samir, Ahmed, Ali and myself) were trying to steal from a grapevine which had appeared, tempting, from behind one of the hedges. Sorry ... I mean, it didn't really quite appear. It was summer, which means the grapes had ripened. The hedge was very high, three metres ... Well, maybe only one metre. But relative to our size, it seemed like three metres ... Anyway, in order to reach the vine, we made a human pyramid. The first one fell – the one standing at the bottom. So the others fell. There was a technical problem. Though I was the strongest, I stood on top of them all, while the one who stood at the bottom had the weakest build. The important thing is that we fell on muddy ground, and so soiled our clothes. Rain had fallen the night before ... No, it can't have been rain, for it was summertime. It doesn't matter. The important thing is that there was water.

We arrived late at the classroom The teacher shook his cane and said, 'Why did God ever create the likes of you? Ten minutes late, your clothes in such a state you look like rats that have come out of filthy dens!'

And the cane swished round in the air.

'And where,' he continued, 'were you, you little devils?'

And the cane, above the horizon, made circles.

'We were helping Old Mustafa move the water pipes in the field,' I said.

I knew that Mustafa was his friend.

'Oh. Is that so?'

'Yes.'

'Sit down then, you monkeys.'

And, laughing to ourselves, we sat down . . . We were saved . . . And that was the first time . . . It was so easy. It didn't hurt me in the least, though we always say it does. In any case, there was no other way of getting rid of the cane circling above.

In order to escape from the house, especially in the summer when chores in the field increased, we would resort to lies of this kind. Tiny little lies – except that they bore fruit amazingly quickly. It was enough to imagine the heaps of boxes that I'd have to move in the field for me to feel extremely exhausted. So, I'd put my hand on my stomach, grimace with pain, and I'd get out of work for that day.

And I was happy . . . I kept that secret to myself, regularly reaping its fruits. I told a lie a day, until I finally discovered how stupid I was. I was oblivious of the many pranks that had been played on me by the devils amongst my colleagues . . .

But when we grew up, the situation took a very complicated form. I used always to believe that the boundaries between falsehood and veracity are so fine that they often go unperceived. And lying remained a means, but now a means towards greater ends. Circumstances sometimes dictated lying as one of the ways leading to safety. Then, things developed. The lie, to be successful, would require premeditated and minute preparations. Consequently, its fruit would be more plentiful, riper, tastier.

And that, my friend, is how boundaries totally disappeared, how things became confused and how the search for truth became an imaginary subject.

I laughed a lot when I discovered that everyone was engaged in the same occupation, doing the same thing, progressing, rising, regressing, going down, in that same mutable fashion.

Take a simple lie which I told in front of a colleague of mine. This time, without a reason, for I had gradually become accustomed to neglecting reasons and justifications. The next day, the lie was published in a modest place in a newspaper of minor circulation. And before I could shake off my dismay, the same story was published in a bigger newspaper, with a wider circulation, in a more prominent place, and under a big headline. One surprise came after the other, and the story was published in all the newspapers. Then, because it was attributed to a 'reliable source', it was broadcast on the radio. Then, on television ... And on television, what a farce! It makes me laugh to this very day ... There, there were real pictures!

And how did it all happen?

I've got used to not asking.

Why? Irrelevant.

Who? None of my business.

This picture was enough to shake my faith in reality. But the journey had not yet come full circle.

Events took a more dramatic turn.

My wife died, you know. She died – that matter brooks no argument. Her life had been a series of lies told by nature. Then nature itself wished to put an end to this game. And so it was.

After that, I got used to lying to my daughter. I would tell her that her mother had gone to the market. Such a lie is silly indeed and is quickly found out Then I said that she had gone to visit the old grandfather in the city. And, to sound credible, I gave her a very lifelike picture of the city. The wide streets. Lamp-posts. Shop-windows. Public gardens. Crowds. Cars. Grandfather's house surrounded by a garden The grapevine climbing the walls. The guava tree. The fountain. The fish pond. The playground. And it was absolutely clear that all these features of the city were imaginary.

With the passing of time, the child discovered the lie, for her mother did not return, and the city was near.

And finally I told her that her mother had gone up into the sky. How?. Just like that. And I described the sky and I described heaven with its rivers and fruits ... Do all people go there? Of course not ... There is hell ... And I described hell, observing the expression of distress on the face of the child who said, 'I'm afraid that mother may be there.'

I then spent days and nights telling her the stories and legends of kings, of jinn and cities and worlds beneath the sea and demons and giants, until the child was totally stricken with dismay and almost struck dumb. She began to see links between natural phenomena on the one hand and parts of and descriptions from the stories and the legends on the other.

And then one day. . .

In the evening I said to the child, 'Tomorrow, I'll be travelling into the city. Would you like me to get you anything?'

The child was quiet and finally said, 'I want to come with you.'

Because I knew that it would be impossible for me to take her along since I was going to spend the day getting important and urgent work done, I said to her, 'No, my love The city is ugly'

In tears, the girl insisted on joining me, and I had no alternative but to lie And so, in a crazed and frantic manner, I said, 'Listen, they eat children there. Especially those with beautiful blonde hair.'

The child cowered in her seat.

'So,' I said maliciously, 'will you come with me?'

Terrified, she said, 'No.'

I travelled to the city, carrying within me not a trace of my lying. I became totally engrossed in work until I became both tired and hungry. I sat in a quiet restaurant under a tree and felt a pleasant numbness creep over me. I closed my eyes, my hand touching the ice cold bottle of beer.

Hearing screams of terror from the other side of the street, my eyes flew open and I stared in front of me. It was a very tall tree. The people in the street surrounded the tree, letting out sounds of approval and joy, their eyes smiling. Right under the tree were four men with cruel features, neither laughing nor screaming. On the tree was a little girl strung up by her hair, letting out terrible squeals of terror, blood running from her face and from the rest of her body. Her voice sent shivers up my spine and I heard my bones make a frightening, cracking sound. One of the four men took a very long knife. My throat became dry and I forgot all about the cold bottle of beer in front of me. The man cut off a big chunk of the girl's flesh and shoved it into his mouth. The blood and saliva were mixed on the man's face. I wanted to scream but couldn't. I wanted to get up but couldn't.

I looked at the child's face for the last time and felt the chair collapse under the weight of my body upon which a new weight had landed... She was my child – my daughter – she of the long blonde hair.

Translated by Nur Elmessiri

The City

Mohamed Tamila

Nobody in the city. Wind and darkness and an old watchman who lit a fire next to the gate of one of the buildings and sat near it. Another old man passed in front of me without a greeting.

The wind grew stronger and a light drizzle began to fall. Hearing a commotion on the second floor, I looked up and saw an old woman standing behind a window, keeping an eye on what was going on in the street.

My hair got wet. Water dripped on to my collar and down my back. A police car hurried past, its wheels splashing the muddy water on to me. I wiped the water and mud off my face with the little rag my wife always takes care to keep in my pocket. The police car stopped twenty metres away from me and reversed till it came in line with me. An old policeman inside it coughed and ordered me to approach the window so that he could check my ID. He asked me my name and age. When I told him I was thirty years old, he exchanged looks of amazement and surprise with his ancient companions, and ordered me into the car. I got in and sat in the back seat next to an elderly policeman who coughed all the way to the police station. As for the driver, who was around eighty years old, he never spoke until it began pouring down with rain. How youthful the sky is, it is still capable of raining – he said something to that effect.

We all stepped out of the car. They led me through a huge gate into a corridor in which a number of ancient men were sleeping. One of them was woken up by our noise. He rose heavily, leaning on a stick, to open a heavy iron door which I realized was a cell door. They shoved me in and slammed the door shut.

I could see nothing. But I heard loud snoring and coughing coming from somewhere in the darkness. Taking a step forward, I stumbled upon some sticks which, I later found, were walking sticks. From the heart of the darkness a hoarse voice ordered me to keep quiet. Then the owner of the voice gave a long cough and went back to sleep. For fear of making any more noise, I stayed in my place, waiting for dawn to break.

The darkness lifted, enabling me to make out the bodies of the prisoners carelessly strewn on the floor of the room. They were asleep, and when it became clear to me that they were all old men, I thought to myself that a man of that age is in dire need of rest. And I felt an overflow of happiness at still being thirty years old.

I did not wait long. Soon enough an ancient policeman came and took me to meet the ancient officer. The officer asked me, 'Do you really claim to be in your thirties?'

'Yes.'

The ancient officer looked at all of those who were in the room and pointed to his head, making the sign one uses to say that someone is mad. Then he gave the order to set me free.

I left the police station quickly. At the great gate, the ancient guard told me, 'Don't forget to visit us again, young man.' And he burst into mocking laughter.

I huddled into my coat and walked along the pavement towards the car park. But the crowds hindered my progress. Hundreds of ancient people were getting out of cars and moving slowly in all directions: some were leaning on walking sticks, some had bent backs, others were actually crawling. Duty required me to help some of them cross the street, and I would have done so, had worry about my wife and small child not made me feel that I should hurry back before they woke up, especially since they knew nothing of what had happened to me.

I got into the taxi and directed the ancient driver to take me as fast as possible to where I lived. The taxi stopped at a traffic light, where a school bus drew to a halt next to us. What amazed me was that all the passengers in the bus were old people well over eighty. When I voiced my amazement to the ancient driver, he pursed his lips as if to say, 'Don't make a fool of me,' and drove on in a nasty temper.

I paid the ancient man the fare. I climbed the stairs to my flat, opened the door and called out for my wife. She did not answer. I rushed to the bedroom, where I was flabbergasted to find an ancient woman who looked like my wife, and an ancient man who looked like my child, asleep on my bed. I recoiled in horror. Then I saw myself in the mirror, and fell to the floor.

Translated by Sahar Hamouda

Nothing

Ghassan Kanafani

It was reported in the news that a soldier on the border
had suddenly opened fire with his gun on the occupied
territory and had been confined to a mental hospital
suffering from a nervous breakdown.

That was the first time that he had heard the term
'nervous breakdown'. He asked the male nurse who was
leading him outside, 'What does a nervous breakdown
mean?'

'It means you're not well,' the nurse replied curtly.

He raised his hand and tapped the side of his head with
his finger asking, 'Here?'

'Yes, there!'

He stood for a short while. He was not sure of anything
and, not knowing what he was supposed to say, he asked
once again, 'A nervous breakdown . . . here?'

'Yes.'

'What does that mean?'

'It means you're not well.'

'How?'

The nurse pulled him violently by the arm and he felt
that he was talking nonsense and had no control over his
tongue. A huge black spider had come to inhabit his
forehead and was building intricate, cruel webs between
his eyes.

'Where are you taking me now?'

'You have to see the boss.'

He tried to stop, but the nurse pushed him on violently. So he continued, 'Tell me, this meeting with the boss, does it have anything to do with the nervous thing here?'

He pointed to the side of his head once more. And the spider went on spinning its web.

'Most likely, yes.'

'Yes what?'

'Hmph . . .'

Once again he felt that, really, he was not well. But he wanted to give, as much as possible, free reign to his tongue.

'Do you know something?'

'What?'

He stood his ground firmly and wagged his finger in the face of the nurse. When the nurse tried to push him on, he stiffened his legs as if in a spasm and refused . . .

'I want to tell you something.'

'What?'

'True, it's a nervous breakdown, but not here.'

'Where then?'

Pointing to his chest, he quietly said, 'Here.'

'A nervous breakdown never happens there.'

'Says who?'

'The doctors.'

'They're crazy.'

He walked on a bit, then stopped and wagged his finger in the face of the nurse once again.

'The doctors are crazy . . . and anyway, this isn't a medical case; it's a military one.'

'Why's this case military?'

'Because I myself am a soldier.'

'And what's the difference?'

'What do you mean?'

Again, the nurse pulled him violently and walked him down the clean silent corridor. The doors on both sides were shut. And the spider had begun to sing while completing its cruel web between his eyes.

'Is he far from here?'

'Who?'

'The boss.'

'At the end of the corridor.'

He was disturbed by the conversation ending so soon and felt that he ought to be talking a lot. An overwhelming desire took him by the temples, shaking him without mercy. The nurse accompanying him insisted on pulling him violently. All his attempts to come to a halt were of no avail.

'Listen, you've tired me out ... Let's stop a while and rest ... Besides, I am, as the doctor said, a sick man.'

The nurse stopped. He sized him up with his eyes for a while, then shook his head firmly, pressing his lips together. In the meantime, he leaned on the wall, following the slow steps of the spider moving about in his forehead, completing its cobweb.

'How did he know that I've got this ... this ... this thing that has to do with the nerves here?'

'The nervous breakdown?'

'Yes ... the nervous breakdown. How did he know?'

'He asked you special questions; they know the illness from the answers.'

'But he didn't ask me many. He asked me two or three times, then, pouring over his register, he began to write. He asked me what I'd felt before the firing and I told him that I didn't feel a single thing. Then he asked what I'd felt after the firing and I told him that I didn't feel a single thing.'

'That's all.'

'Oh, no. He was greatly disappointed when I told him "nothing". He wanted to write and I really wanted to help him. So I said ...'

'What did you say?'

'I told him that after the shooting, I'd felt only one thing:

that the cartridge clip runs out too soon.'

'You really felt that?'

He shook his head sadly. The spider had finished spinning its home and was sitting in the centre, stretching its many arms, in search of a fly.

'Oh, yes! You can't imagine how dazzling it was! One pull of the trigger and all is over. They only let us carry one clip.'

'Let's go.'

He pulled him by the arm and walked on with him. For the first time since he had received the hard blow on the nape of his neck, and the military car had taken him to the hospital, he felt intimacy. Basking in that comfortable feeling, he noticed that they had stripped him of his military uniform and clothed him in strange attire. But he did not want to guess when that had happened.

'You killed two.'

'Who?'

'You, when you fired, you killed two of them.'

'And what's surprising about that? When one fires shots, they're aimed at something.'

'You meant to?'

'Humph! What do you think?'

'I thought it was a nervous breakdown.'

'What's the difference?'

'The difference is that you don't mean to do it when you have a nervous breakdown.'

He halted suddenly. The netting of the spider's home was torn. It shook in its shelter, but soon enough it was back obstinately repairing the damage done to its web.

'So they think I didn't do it on purpose?'

'Yes.'

'Yes? I *did* do it on purpose.'

'If you say this in front of them they'll throw you in prison. You'd do well to hold your tongue.'

Frantic, ferocious, the spider worked on, causing a clamour in his forehead. It seemed to him that he was about to fall. The long corridor took one long spin around itself and then went back to where it had been.

'Why do they want me to say that I didn't do it on purpose?'

'Because what you did isn't the right thing to do.'

He planted his feet firmly on the ground. The nurse pulled him on, but he pulled his arm back violently. More filaments in the spider's home were torn.

'Do you want me to tell you something?'

'No! I just want you to walk with me. We've wasted enough time . . .'

'I won't move before I tell you something.'

'Fine. Say it then.'

'I'm ill with that nervous thing because I fired my gun on purpose . . . Isn't that so?'

'Yes.'

More filaments in the spider's home were torn, and the black insect became more frantic in its attempt to mend the rent. He went on, 'And others don't have that serious thing that has to do with the nerves because they don't shoot on purpose. Isn't that right?'

'Yes. What are you trying to say?'

'What am I trying to say? Humph! Nothing... Nothing...'

He walked on quickly. His big feet hit the floor, causing his huge body to sway. The spider in his forehead was shaking, the web getting violently torn. Then he shouted: 'Listen, are you sure that this is right?'

'What is?'

'What you've just said about the nerves thing.'

'Of course. Of course.'

He looked the nurse over carefully. The spider was beginning to fade away. Suddenly, all traces of the spider's interwoven web disappeared and the inside of his forehead became as clear as a white marble slab.

'Fine. Let's go to the boss!'

Translated by Randa Elgeyoushi

The Crucified Sheep

Ghassan Kanafani

All the space that stretched out endlessly before my eyes
was burning under the blazing summer sun. Dust beat
ceaselessly against the car window. Whenever I turned
my gaze to the faces of my travelling companions, I clearly
felt the harshness of our trip. Their hair was white with
dust; even their eyelashes were washed with bitter milk.
They were panting and into the dust on their faces sweat
had dug channels that branched into small streams and
trickled down their necks.

Those despicable sentences which had been entertaining me ever since we began our trip began to buzz
again in my ears.

'This is a strange trip! Today it is nothing but a tragedy,
and tomorrow we shall say it was an adventure.'

The long line of cars ran ovee the sandy winding road,
cutting through the silence of the desert like a vein of
madness swallowed up by the depths.

A fit of philosophizing poured from my exhausted
companions' lips.

'There is no truth in the world. So?'

'Yes. We have been condemned to fall inside our minds
and find nothing to hold on to. Truth is always with
others. As for ourselves, we are nothing but doubt itself.'

'Sometimes it seems to me that the man who believes
deeply in ideals is closer than anyone else to abandoning

his faith, for he has learnt to doubt with sincerity.'

These words seemed to me to have no meaning whatsoever. Once a man finds that things exist, the question of their justification becomes pointless. And we *had* seen them – that's all that matters to me.

'Is it the bedouin who's made your head teem with all this philosophy?'

'Oh, the bedouin! I'd almost forgotten him. It might have been the bedouin. It may be this damned heat. I don't know.'

I know it's only the bedouin. For when an intellectual is taught a small lesson by a bedouin lost in the Empty Quarter, he feels some shame. My colleague, the doctor, tries to attribute his headache to the sun. No – it is the bedouin. And no matter how hard the car tried to distance itself from the spot where we had left him, we would still be ruthlessly locked to those sharp eyes that kept following our car until they were concealed by the scorching heat and the dust. I wanted to stop listening to my companions' conversation, but, within these walls, shaking continuously, I had no other entertainment.

'This philosophizing hasn't cleared out of your mind since we left Kuwait. Do you remember telling me that being chosen to accompany the pilgrimage was the biggest farce of your life?'

'Well! But I did come. I've lived all my life totally without faith. Choosing me to be one of the pilgrims' doctors was tantamount to forcing me into pilgrimage. Can you imagine that?'

'I can well imagine it. You usually spend these days in Cairo or Lebanon or maybe in Switzerland. But to spend them in this hell stretching endlessly must be most disturbing for you. As for me . . .'

'You adore trips! What you're longing for is for the car to break down and for us to find ourselves forced to go on by crawling over this molten glass. Aren't you longing for all this to happen so that one day, puffed up like a crazy cock, you can tell the story to some girls?'

The opinions of this doctor disturb me a lot. But in spite of that, he knows how to trap others. His colleague burst out laughing and he accepted both his defeat and the implicit compliment. Tell the story of his adventures to some girls! How strange! Wonder what he will tell them this time? Most likely he'll begin the conversation this way:

'Honest to God! We saw him there. He was right in the middle of the desert. The sun was fierce, scorching the sand, but he was standing there, calm and gentle. Where did he come from? Nobody knows. How did he get there? Nobody knows. What was he looking for? Most probably for water for his scrawny sheep. He was looking after nine lean sheep grazing on desert thorns . . . and he was just standing there.'

If he began this way he would attract the seated women's attention. One of the guests would offer him a cigarette so that he would get into the conversation even more. Maybe one of the women, totally engrossed in the amusing story, would spill a drop or two of her drink on her dress. And he, there's no doubt that, at that moment, he would be ecstatic . . . and questions would fall upon him from all sides.

'What was he doing there?' 'Did he look well built?' 'He was dark, wasn't he?' 'Did you talk to him?' 'Was he not armed?' 'You say half mad?' 'How can one bedouin obstruct a large convoy of cars?' 'The amazing thing is that he managed to stop it!' 'Did he speak classical Arabic?'

As for him, he would get more and more puffed up as he tried to slow down the gush of their enthusiasm.

'Why are you so astonished? In that desert, so remote from the world, a travelling doctor can see anything. It seems strange to you, now. But for us it was perfectly normal. In those days, nothing appeared unusual in our eyes. So, when we saw him standing there, alone except for his nine lean sheep, it didn't surprise or astonish anyone.'

That's what he would say, telling the story. But when we saw it together, when we stared together through the dusty car window, we were astonished. In the distance he seemed small, surrounded by nine black spots in the yellow of the blazing sand. I heard a voice from behind, 'It looks like a man crucified in the middle of this strange desert.'

His arms were indeed stretched in a way that was almost horizontal, but he was, in spite of that, standing on the ground. As the car came closer, our astonishment dwindled bit by bit, to be replaced by something like curiosity, for from the top of a small hill we saw him clearly.

A dark bedouin staring coldly, as if he were used to seeing such sights all the time. Arms outstretched over an ancient gun resting across his shoulders and the back of his neck. Dressed in an old *keffiya* thrown carelessly on his head and an old garment offering protection against neither sun nor dust. His nine sheep lay around him, panting – we could hear the whistling of their breath – obviously spent by the heat.

As the cars slowed down and came to a stop next to him, it seemed that a strange attack of fever was what had suggested to me that this man's presence was possible . . . distant from everything . . . just some lean sheep for company and an ancient gun stretched across his shoulders. I thought – for an instant – that I had to touch him with my fingers to convince myself that he was both present and possible.

A voice behind me called out cheerfully, but also with fear, 'Here's a myth from Sparta. Man and god in one place. Wonder what he's doing here?'

'Worshipping,' the other doctor answered him coolly.

The driver had got out and we heard their conversation through the car window.

'You're bound for pilgrimage, aren't you?'

'Yes. Do you want any supplies?'

We got out of the car too and headed towards him. His eyes held something inexplicable. It seemed he didn't want anything except for us to leave him be.

'I don't want any supplies. I don't eat much.'

'What are you doing here?' asked a voice behind me. A surprised amazement shone in the bedouin's eyes as if the question were meaningless. Then he murmured, 'I'm putting these out to graze.'

'These? What can you find here for them to graze on?'

'Thorns. They're still somewhat soft.'

'But your sheep look tired.'

He looked at them, as though he were seeing them for the first time. A hard spark of pain shone in his eyes. He shook his head.

'They are thirsty.'

'Then give them to drink.'

'I have no water. And I haven't had a single drop all day long.'

Grief spread in his eyes till it took possession of everything and it seemed to me that he was about to cry. But the loudmouth behind me still wanted to go on with his questions, 'And you? Aren't you thirsty?'

'Me?'

He shook his head again and, arms still stretched out across the gun, went on: 'I don't matter. But these poor things are thirsty.'

'How do you eat here?'

'I swallow some milk from their teats every morning – but they are thirsty.'

'When are you going back to your people?'

He curled his lip, shook his head silently, and stared once more at his sheep lying on the ground. Then he whispered, 'I don't matter. But these poor things are thirsty.' Then he turned towards us with pleading eyes and shouted imploringly, 'Don't you have any water for these poor things?'

'No, I swear . . .' the driver replied. 'We don't have much water. But if you want we can give you some to drink.'

The bedouin ignored the offer and asked, nodding towards the car loaded with water barrels.

'Isn't that water?'

'Yes, it's water. But it's for the cars.'

'Water for the cars?' he asked in surprise, and the driver replied, 'Cars always need water.'

'But the sheep are thirsty. They may even die.'

He stared apprehensively at the barrels, then shook his head as if he would never understand, and repeated, 'The sheep are thirsty. They may even die.'

'If you want, we can give you water to drink.'

'I want water for my sheep. Can't you see they're thirsty?'

'Do you want food?'

He shook his head once again. Moving his eyes across each and every one of our faces, he beseeched us in a distressed voice, 'Can't you see they're about to die? They're thirsty.'

'But we can't give you any water.'

'Why not?'

'The cars . . .'

'The cars? Are all these cars worth one of my sheep?' For a second it seemed like a new joke. Then the look of grief in his sharp eyes brought us back to the bitterness of the situation.

'Are your people very far from here?'

He waved his hand, from over his gun behind his back, and said dully, 'Far . . .'

'And now what will you do?'

He shrugged his shoulders again, and stared at his sheep, then at our faces and, calmly, he turned around and, giving us his back, looked out across the desert.

When the car engines started up again, we heard the driver yell, making him the last offer.

'We're ready to give you what you want to eat and drink. Don't you want that?'

Through the dusty car windows we saw him turn around to face us, crucified on his gun as we'd always seen him. His trembling lips called out, 'They're thirsty. They may even die this evening.'

The cars moved, and the crucified man gradually diminished in the distance until he disappeared into the heat and dust.

The fit of philosophizing still kept its hold over the minds of my companions in the back seat. I found myself forced to repeat to myself those despicable sentences that had been tormenting my mind for a long time.

'This is a strange trip. Today it is nothing but a tragedy, and tomorrow we shall say it was an adventure.'

Translated by Sahar Hamouda

A Conversation

Jamal Naji

I saw the man with the coarse coat and the cruelly pursed lips as soon as I got on the bus. Approaching him, I greeted him once within earshot, hoping that he would draw in his legs and his arms, which were stretched out around an open newspaper. More than this, I even made a show of looking around the bus, so that the man would realize that there were no other empty seats except for the one next to him. And still the man paid no attention. I tried to think of a reason why he should deign not to return my greeting.

Maybe, I thought, he is intent on some particularly important piece of news, and so, with some difficulty, I squeezed in next to him. I assumed, naturally, that my neighbour would soon draw in his limbs, and I would be allowed to sit, as was my right, comfortably. Except he had different ideas, the proof being that the bus moved off without his attempting to move. He paid no attention to the fidgeting and sighing through which I attempted to make him aware of my shrunken presence.

His shameless way of ignoring me infuriated me, so I spoke up politely.

'If you don't mind,' I said, 'please move over a little, so that I might sit comfortably.'

I was answered in perfect, classical Arabic, in a strangely icy manner.

'I am not prepared to sacrifice my comfort for you.'

The man closed his lips tightly, as if to eradicate any trace of the compromise he had just made in deigning to speak to me. And the truth was that his hard voice had filled me with a sense of anxiety that grew stronger when I glimpsed the skin of his hand, drawn tightly around a protruding wrist. Yet still I was not deterred from asking once again for my rightful share of the seat. I pulled myself together and spoke to him.

'Fine, mister, and what about my comfort?'

'I am not responsible for your comfort.'

'But you have achieved your comfort at the expense of mine.'

I was becoming increasingly agitated and annoyed.

He replied in the same, hard voice, 'So be it. The important thing is that I am comfortable.'

What compounded my astonishment was that the man did not even bother to look at me while making these unqualified statements but instead continued to look at the newspaper with two hard glass eyes.

'But my comfort is important too. Don't you see that you're only thinking of yourself?'

He answered, coldly, without turning to me, 'And what is wrong with that?'

Wrong? I asked myself. I decided that since he was thinking along such lines there was no question of a fist fight between the man and myself. So, intending to provoke him, I dared to say, 'What is wrong is that he who doesn't think of others is quite obviously selfish.'

I expected a sharp reaction to this provocation; rather I was dumbfounded by the cold way in which he said, 'What is wrong with a person being selfish?'

'Selfishness is a bad quality.'

'All right, if it makes you feel better: I am bad. And what is wrong with that?'

'Doesn't it bother you to be bad?'

He rolled his head as if to say no.

A Conversation

Filled with horror, I asked him, 'Why? Why doesn't it bother you?'

'Because my comfort is more important. As to being bad, that remains a theoretical problem that bears no relation to my comfort.'

'Fair enough. And how in your situation do you distinguish between theory and practice?'

'In practice, I am comfortable sitting as I am. In theory, I am bad.'

In that bus, a heated discussion occurred between us about the concepts of selfishness, theory and practice, right and wrong, which might have lasted till the Day of Judgment had I not suddenly turned to see through the windows my house receding into the distance. I sprang to my feet as if stung and felt my entire body expand, returning to its normal condition after the contraction of the journey. But before I left my seat I threw a question into the face of the man, 'Do you realize,' I said, 'that you are the worst creature I have ever met?'

He looked at me for the first time, and smiling – also perhaps for the first time in his life – he said, 'Remember that during the course of this conversation you forgot entirely your right to share the seat with me.'

Translated by Magda Amin and Nur Elmessiri

154

Flying Carpet

Riyad Baidas

A blue Fiat 127 stopped beside me. The driver leaned out
and asked in Hebrew the way to Kfar Ata. I gave him
directions but he was unable to visualize all the winding,
narrow roads. As I was on my way there myself, I asked if I
could travel with him and show him the way. He did not
object, but then neither did he show any enthusiasm. He
merely nodded in assent and after a moment's thought, I
found myself in the front seat beside him. I asked about
his destination and he said he was on his way to Haifa. I
was glad and said I would travel with him to Haifa.

The way to Kfar Ata is full of crossroads. I was attentive
the whole time and gave him directions as best I could.

When we were on the outskirts of the city, he said, 'Do
you have many friends?'

'Why?' I asked with a smile.

Trying to break the ice, he said, 'I noticed you greeting
quite a few people. Where I come from, it's different. You
could run into your next-door neighbour and not say
hello.'

Laughing, I responded, 'Well, actually, I think I misled
you. Very soon, we'll be just like you. Those you saw me
greet aren't my friends. They're acquaintances, no more,
no less.'

He did not seem to grasp properly what I had just said.
Examining me furtively he asked, 'But there must be some
stronger tie between you?'

When I noticed him looking me over, I realized that I had made a mistake in asking him for a lift. The man was talking more than was necessary in order to keep himself entertained and to take his mind off things.

'I just know these people . . . that's all there is to it. In the village, you know everybody, though you may not be friends with them.'

He gave a sullen smile and glanced out of the window, then turned to me and said, 'But your town is not a village.'

'Nor is it a city either,' I interjected.

'Do you know Hilmy?' he asked. 'I went to see him . . . he's the tile-layer who's fixing the floor tiles in my new house. I found his house with difficulty. I'd gone with the house number, so people laughed at me. But when I said Hilmy the tile-layer, they immediately knew who I was talking about.'

Laughing, I said in a jest, 'Every one of us is a Hilmy.'

He seemed astonished. 'What do you mean?' he asked thoughtfully.

'What do you need a house number for?' I said. 'Where I come from, no one knows, let alone uses, these numbers – that is, if the houses are numbered in the first place.'

The man was stocky, with chestnut hair and a round white face. He had black sunglasses on and was dressed in light sports clothes. His almost clownish movements indicated that he was not comfortable about my travelling with him. His questions and incessant chatter betrayed so much tension and suspicion that I started to become irritated. But I controlled myself and refrained from asking him to stop and let me out. I did my best to ignore his movements and go on with the trip to see what might happen, especially since his tension had mounted to an extraordinary degree. When he shifted gears, his trembling hand would knock against my left knee in agitated, involuntary movements and he would apologize and swallow in embarrassment.

The road stretched ahead of him as clear as an open

palm and he would easily have been able to continue his journey alone, without any difficulties. He no longer needed me to guide him.

'Is there something wrong with the car?' I asked.

He was taken aback and pursed his lips. 'No, why do you ask?'

'I meant the gears,' I said.

He did not get my meaning. Just when I was about to ask him to drop me off, he enquired in an odd tone, 'Do you work in Haifa?'

'I live and work in Haifa.'

'Where do you live?'

'In Reimz.'*

He turned to me in amazement as though he had not expected me to be living in such a district. Trying to cover up what his expression had betrayed, he said, 'In Reimz? It's such a lovely district.'

Refusing to let his shocked expression disturb me, I replied, 'It certainly is a lovely district. Still, I am unable to spend Friday and Saturday mornings there.'

'Why?'

Laughing, I explained, 'Friday afternoons, after four, I feel suffocated in a way that is hard to explain.'

He lifted his glasses revealing two blue inquisitive eyes and asked with interest, 'Why is that so?'

'It's a very personal feeling. All movement dies down. I find myself wondering if all the people of Haifa desert the city on Friday evenings. And so I feel that everything is getting to me and I can't stay. I escape the city and return on Saturday afternoon.'

'And what happens on Saturday afternoon?'

I examined him for a moment, in boredom, then replied, 'The dead silence comes to an end and life slowly flows back into things.'

'What a strange feeling.'

*Reimz is a Jewish suburb

A heavy silence enveloped the car. I tried to keep myself entertained one way or another. To read a book in someone's car, I realized, would be extremely rude. I turned to him and noticed that he was examining the black plastic bag in which I had packed some of my things. To allay his suspicions, I lifted the bag under his eye and opened it, pretending I was looking for something. I pulled out an Arsène Lupin book, skimmed through it and then returned it to the bag. Then I pulled out two date cakes and offered him one. He declined, saying he never ate cakes. I devoured one and started turning the other over in my hand while he glanced in my direction every now and then. I brought the second cake to my mouth and ate it in one bite, then leaned back in my seat, trying to think of some way to relieve myself of the burden of his gaze. I considered asking whether he minded my travelling with him, but refrained for fear that I might be wrong or be behaving rashly and would regret it. I remained silent. His hand travelled towards the tape recorder and he pressed a button. The low strains of the music relieved the oppressive atmosphere. But then he put out his hand again and switched off the tape recorder. I did not know what to make of him.

'There is not much traffic on the roads on Saturdays,' he said glancing towards me.

I agreed, adding, 'But the scenery changes on Saturday mornings.'

'How is that?' he enquired with great interest.

I realized that I had to change the tedious course of the conversation and clear the air of the tension which was poisoning it. With suppressed anger, I commented, 'Any slight change alters the nature of the scenery.'

With obvious irritation, he retorted, 'I envy you your Hebrew. But I still can't understand what you're trying to say.'

'Me of all people,' I answered coldly, 'my Hebrew is weak.'

'Weak,' he broke in, 'I wish my Arabic were as fluent as your Hebrew.'

'You could always study Arabic,' I answered.

'It's too late.' He seemed upset. 'I should have studied it a long time ago. Had I learned Arabic, I would have been able to imagine what's going on inside your head.'

'That would be difficult,' I answered.

'Why?'

'Learning a language is one thing but what's going on inside my head is another.'

'Maybe. But, tell me, how does the scenery change on Saturdays?'

I laughed and he seemed disturbed. So I said, 'If you change the position of some object or other in your home, that alters the whole look and appearance of the house. Doesn't it?'

'Yes, it does.'

'Well, then, the nearly deserted streets on Saturday alter the scenery.'

'But the scenery is the same.'

'Movement and noise change the look of things.'

'I don't understand you.'

'Another example. You have a garage. Now if you put a car in the garage, the garage looks different from when it's empty. Right?'

'You mean emptiness and fullness.'

'Not exactly. Noise mars the beauty of scenery.'

'I don't think I've grasped it completely; but tell me, what do you prefer?'

'Fullness.'

'Why?'

'It creates closeness.'

'And what has closeness got to do with all this?'

'It is you and I,' I went on philosophically, 'who create closeness and not closeness that creates us. What do you think about that?'

He sat there reflecting, without uttering a word. I went

on apologetically, 'Oh, I don't mean closeness between me and you, we hardly know each other. I apologize if you got my meaning wrong. But closeness between people, regardless of where they come from, is vitally important.'

'True!' he said, obviously fed up with the conversation. Then he fell silent as though borrowing time to think about what I had just said. But he loosened his belt, then tightened it again, without saying a word. I kept my eye on the road and the signs ahead of me. A few minutes of stifling silence passed, then he said, 'We're quite close to Haifa. The way is easy now.'

To prevent the tense silence from descending again, I said, 'Yes, the way is easy. Have you heard about the jumbo planes? You must have heard about them.'

Trying to avoid those suspicious looks taut with discontent, I added with a smile, 'Look! It's a blessing to be able to look around you. I can't imagine how anyone can resist the beauty of this view. These plains stretching all around us, the greenery, the pastures and all these farm animals are so calming. How can one weary of these scenes which sing to and intoxicate the anxious soul?'

'Have you gone mad?' he broke in. 'Where do you see all that? What's up with you?'

I leaned back in despair. Ignoring his mutterings, his glances and his confusion, I went on: 'The branches of the trees bend under the abundance of fruit and the birds do not cease chirping, day in and day out. The sun never sets on this region. And people walking in groups or on their own, they are so close to one another, so happy, unrestrained! Look, just look at that lady over there, mutton dressed as lamb, her hair dyed in an effort to look young. See how she kisses her husband – an eternal kiss. They must be both over a hundred, but love rejuvenates the elderly. Blessed is passionate love! Why don't you stop a while so that we can take our fill of this lovely scene. Who would have believed that this spot would come to hold such enchanting sights? Who would have believed that the peace-loving would live in this vast area? Stop a while and look at this unique scene; the sky embraces the land in this spot where people ascend and descend as though treading on firm ground. Is this paradise? Oh, the glory of it all!'

The man turned and stared at me in panic, 'For goodness sake! What's come over you? Is this some kind of a joke? If it is, then that's OK. If you're a poet, then that's OK, too.'

I retorted, annoyed, 'The problem is that you are interrupting me at the height of this beautiful moment. Do you realize what this means? You cannot see what I see. You amaze me. What amazes me is that you should be apparently so oblivious of such beautiful sights. Take this camel, for example. He walks slowly on the grass and sadly looks around, unappreciative of the value of beauty and comfort. In the midst of heaven, he seeks the desert. He looks around him, examining the place and wishing, deep down, that it should all turn into desert. See that tiger there? It is looking for prey, although there are tons of fresh meat all around it. All this greenery does not attract your attention; all this flowing water has no effect on you; all this beauty born of the marriage of earth and sky leaves you unmoved. Why is that so?'

Nor would I let him speak. Instead, smiling very happily, I went on: 'Look at these wonderful little bicycles. To prevent fatal accidents, they don't allow cars to pass through this area. Around here, human life is valued above all things. And the lion dwells in peace with the people. Isn't that beautiful? Take a look, but be careful not to crash into anything. We're almost there. This spot will not be visible to you each time. So please make sure you don't miss seeing it. Stop for a while and look carefully. And in the evening, tell your family about all that has happened to you on this special day. Haste is an ungodly thing and we can always get there fast. But stop a while and look on. Sense all this harmony and closeness. Have you actually stopped? Now this is the unexpected change. Do you understand? Had this spot been empty, you would not have seen all that you have seen. Your eyes would have beheld a different sight, whereas now the spot is teeming with all different kinds of trees and grass and people and animals. Are you aware of the difference? Closeness and contact and green grass and tranquillity all create this harmony. Have you now understood it all?'

All at once he had halted at the wayside and now he yelled angrily, 'I see nothing. I've put up with you and I've put up with your stupidities, but I've had enough. Get it?'

I know not how the flying carpet approached, carried us up and took us to Haifa in the wink of an eye.

Translated by Hala Halim and Nur Elmessiri

The Shoes

Mohamed Tamila

It was cold . . .

When my mother ladled the water out of the barrel to prepare the tea, the pot knocked against a layer of ice, so she told me, 'You can't go to school in those clothes. Wait till I get you your new coat and shoes.'

She brought a dark ladies' coat and a pair of boots out of the bottom of the clothes chest, saying, 'I bought these things yesterday from a travelling peddler. They're new, as you can see.'

My mother put me into the enormous coat, and started fastening the buttons so that no air would get through to my chest.

'Mother, it stinks.'

'Turn round so that I can see. Excellent. Here, take the boots.'

My small feet quickly plunged into the hollow of the boots which reached up to my knees.

'I can't walk in these large boots.'

'They're better than sandals, at any rate. Come on, tie up the laces.'

'But they've got holes in them.'

'They're excellent. I bought them for thirty piastres. Come on, show me what you look like now.'

My mother laughed when she saw me stumbling around the room, but she quickly made up for it by saying,

163

'Never mind, my darling. The cold is merciless. But keep the coat clean, and if it rains, hold up the hem so that it doesn't get splattered with mud.'

On the way to school it rained and the wind beat against my face. I found it difficult to move, for the coat dragged along the ground and the boots needed extra effort for each step.I tried to lift the hem of the coat as my mother had advised, but my satchel fell into a small puddle. The rain was pelting down and the wind was blowing against me. I couldn't see in front of me. The water had trickled through the collar of the coat down my back. I was feeling extremely cold, but I didn't care, because I was thinking, 'What if the other pupils see me looking like this? I'd be an absolute laughing stock. We shouldn't be wearing women's clothes.'

I thought of going back home, but it was only a thought. I thought of getting rid of the coat and shoes once and for all. That, too, was only a thought. I made up my mind at last. I would put the coat and shoes somewhere and go to school without them. I looked around me, there was no one in sight. I dug under an odd-shaped rock and hid the coat and boots. I felt relieved as if I had got rid of a heavy burden. I waded into the water barefoot. So what? There are plenty of children who go to school barefoot. It isn't something to be ashamed of. I raced on as fast as I could, feeling as lively as usual.

There were about seventy of us pupils in a small room. The windows were without panes; the wind whistled about the room; the pupils huddled together for warmth; the teacher read out of the English book that lesson about Samir and Salma's visit to London.

The teacher was late for the second lesson. The feet of those of us who were unshod were on the verge of freezing. The principal came in and told us, 'You will leave in an orderly fashion to meet the committee in the administration area.'

Committee? What did the committee want of us? We

felt terribly frightened, and wondered among ourselves whether any of us had done something to bring this committee upon us. To maintain discipline, they let us out one by one.

We waited to hear the howls of the first one to leave, expecting him to be given a sound beating. We were surprised when the first pupil returned carrying a new pair of shoes under his arm. He informed us that the committee was made up of three men and a mountain of new shoes. We didn't believe him of course. The second pupil returned and he, too, had received a pair of shoes. Chaos broke out as the pupils jumped around for joy.

My turn came. I hurried as fast as I could to the administration area. I did find myself in front of a mountain of shoes. One of the men asked me, 'What size are your feet?'

'Eh?'

Annoyed, he asked again, 'What size are your feet?'

I didn't know that feet had sizes. But I'd once heard that one of our relatives had asked his brother who was going to Saudi Arabia to get him a pair of shoes, size 42, so I immediately said, 'I am size 42.'

The man gave me a pair of shoes. I went back to class proud of having known the correct answer. The pupils had put on their new shoes and were stamping on the floor. I tried mine on, but my small feet sank all the way down to the bottom. I tried again, and realized that they were much larger even than that ladies' pair. I could have exploded with frustration. I thought of going back to the committee, but was afraid that they would confiscate the shoes altogether. The pupils were busy with their shoes and so no one noticed my catastrophe. I buried my head in my hands and wept.

On the way back, I didn't feel like putting the shoes on for fear of the pupils' mockery. I tried to look as happy as they did. It was raining, so one of them asked me, 'You idiot, how come you walk barefoot when you've now got some shoes?'

I replied, 'I'll keep them for the next feast.'

He thought for a while, seeming to like the idea, then moved off.

My tears mingled with the rain. I no longer cared about the wind blowing in my face, or the water soaking my clothes. I went to the rock under which I'd hidden the ladies' coat and shoes. I put them on quickly; then, scared of my mother's reproaches should she discover my failure, I hid the new pair under the rock, saying to myself, 'I'll come back for them when I'm older.'

I liked the idea and smiled, for my misery had lifted.

Translated by Sahar Hamouda

The Slope

Ghassan Kanafani

Mr Muhsen walked slowly and reluctantly down the long corridor that led to his classroom. It was his first experience of the world of teaching, and because he didn't know exactly what he was supposed to do when he entered the class, he was trying desperately to put the moment off for as long as possible.

The previous night he had tossed and turned in his bed thinking till daybreak about the matter. It wasn't at all easy to stand up in front of people . . . why do it? To teach them! Who are you to do that? You've lived all your miserable life without anyone ever teaching you anything useful. Do you think you can teach people anything that might be of use to them? You used to believe that school was the last place a man could learn about life, so what do you think now, now that you have become a teacher in one?

In the morning he took himself off to the principal's office and sat there listening to the other teachers talking about the matter which was on his mind, but from another angle . . .

'What on earth are we going to do in the classrooms if the youngsters have no books?'

The principal answered briskly, 'A competent teacher knows how to keep his class busy without books!' He continued slyly, 'Ask one of the children to occupy

167

class time if you aren't able . . .'

Mr Muhsen said to himself, 'This looks like the kind of principal who wants to teach his teachers a lesson about discipline and obedience right from the word go. He collected the fees only last week and already he wants to collect our souls.'

He gulped down his tea and stood up.

The long corridor filled with the din of screaming children. Mr Muhsen, with each heavy step, felt he was being sucked into a worthless future full of noise and nonsense . . . noise and nonsense and nothing else!

'I've got a nice story, sir! . . .' a child crammed into the back bench called out, thus providing a reasonable solution to the confused situation. Before Mr Muhsen could agree to the suggestion, the child had come to the front of the class and was now facing his mates, wearing short trousers that were too wide for him and a shirt made from fabric that an old woman might wear. His thick black hair hung down to his eyebrows . . .

My father was a good man . . . His hair had gone grey and he only had one eye. As for the other eye, he had poked it out himself while he was stitching the thick sole of a fat man's shoe. He was bent over the shoe struggling to get the big needle into the sole, but the sole was very tough. He pushed as hard as he could but it was no use. He pushed harder, still no use. Then he lifted the shoe to his chest and pushed with all his might. The needle shot out of the other side right into his eye.

'My father was a good man. His beard wasn't long but it wasn't short either. He used to work a lot and he was good at his job. He always had a lot of shoes to repair and make wearable again.

'But my father didn't have a good shop, and no one used to help him in his work. His shop was no more than a box made of wood, sheets of metal and cardboard. It was only big enough for him, a few nails, the shoes and a last. Apart from that there wasn't even room for a fly and the customers had to stand outside the box if they wanted their shoes repaired . . .

'This box stood at the bottom of a hill at the top of which was a rich man's palace. It was impossible for anyone to know where the box was if they looked for it from the balcony of the rich man's palace. That was because grass had grown in the dirt on top of it. So my father wasn't worried that the owner of the palace would discover his hiding place and throw him out. The owner of the palace never went out of his palace and servants used to deliver everything he desired to his palace. They agreed with my father to keep his secret from their master in exchange for which he repaired their shoes.

'My father kept at his work without fear or hesitation and people discovered that he was so skilful in fixing shoes that he made them look as good as new. And that was why more and more shoes came to him every day. He used to spend the whole day and half of the night working non-stop. He would say to my mother, "Tomorrow the children will go to school."

'And my mother would say to him, "And you'll be able to take a bit of a rest from all that work."'

The child went back to his place, but his classmates didn't say a word. Mr Muhsen exclaimed, 'Why don't you give a round of applause to your friend, didn't you like the story?'

'We want to hear the rest . . .'

'Is there some more to your story?'

'About a month or so ago, so much work piled up that he was no longer able to come home. My mother would tell us that he was working day and night without leaving his box, that he had no time to go out. And the rich man would spend all day and all night sitting on his balcony eating bananas and oranges and almonds and walnuts and would throw the shells and the peel over the edge of the balcony of his palace to the bottom of the hill. One morning the hill filled up with shells and peel and the servants couldn't find my father's box under it all. My mother said that, as ever, he was so absorbed in his work that he hadn't noticed all the stuff that was being thrown on top of his box. In all probability he is still sitting there working hard to repair the shoes he has so that he can finish and deliver them on time and then come home ... but I think he dies there.'

The pupils clapped and the child went back to his place and sat down quietly. Sixty brightly shining pairs of eyes focused once again on Mr Muhsen ...

Mr Muhsen took the child to the principal's room. On the way he asked him, 'Do you really think your father has died?'

'My father doesn't die. I just said that so I could finish the story. If I hadn't it wouldn't ever have finished. In a few months it will be summer. The sun will dry the piles of peel and shells and lighten their weight. My father will be able to push them to one side and hurry back home ...'

Mr Muhsen reached the principal's room and said to him, 'I have an exceptional child in my class. I think he's a genius. Let him tell you the story of his father ...'

'What's the story of your father?'

'His shop was very small and he was brilliant. One day, word of his great skill reached the owner of the palace which looked out over his small shop. He sent my father all his old shoes to repair and make new again. It took the servants two full days to take the shoes to the small shop and by the time they had finished delivering them, my father had suffocated under the great pile, for his shop wasn't big enough for all those shoes ...'

The principal put his thumb in his waistcoat pocket, thought for a moment, then said, 'This is a crazy child. We'll have to send him to another school.'

The child said, 'But I'm not crazy. Go to the rich man's palace and look at his shoes and you'll find bits of my father's flesh on them. You might even find his eyes or his nose on the sole of some shoe ... Go and have a look ...'

The principal said, 'I believe the child is mad.'

Mr Muhsen answered, 'But he isn't mad. I myself have had my shoes repaired by his father, and when I went back to have them repaired again they told me he'd died.'

'How did he die?'

'He was nailing a sole to an old shoe. That day he'd knocked a lot of nails into that particular shoe to make it really strong. When he finished he realized he'd nailed his fingers between the shoe and the last; imagine! He was so strong that he was able to pierce the metal last with his nails. And when he tried to get up he couldn't. He was stuck fast to the last. The passers-by refused to help him, so there he remained fixed until he died . . .'

The principal looked at Mr Muhsen again. He was standing there next to the child, so close in fact that the two of them seemed as one. The principal shook his head a few times without saying anything, then went and sat down in his comfortable leather chair and started going through some papers. From time to time he glanced at Mr Muhsen and the child out of the corner of his eye.

Translated by Anthony Calderbank

V

Death-in-Life/Life-in-Death

At Last the Almond Blossomed

Emile Habibi

Spring, take me back to my homeland
Even as a flower

A song sung by Fairuz

'In the romantic years of my youth, I read Dickens's novel *A Tale of Two Cities*. I idolized Sidney Carton as the hero who gave his life to save the husband of the woman he loved by putting on the husband's clothes and taking his place in the Bastille, beneath the blade of the guillotine.

'But like everyone else, none of my heroes have been able to resist the trials of adversity. Rather, they have risen and fallen as life itself, until now there remains only Hugo's philosopher Gringoir, that miserable rogue in *The Hunchback of Notre Dame*, who was also asked to sacrifice himself (in order to rescue Esmeralda, the beautiful gypsy) but refused. When questioned as to what made him so attached to life, he replied, "My greatest joy is spending every day from morning till night with the genius who is me. It's wonderful."'

'And Arabism?'

'Are you going to tell me off and be sarcastic after we've been apart for twenty years?'

That was exactly what I had in mind when I reminded Mister M of Arabism. His unexpected night visit had

175

astonished me, and raised my doubts. He had asked me to listen to him patiently.

We had been close friends at preparatory and secondary school. Together we had set up the first secret society in our school to fight the British. Its membership consisted only of the two founding members, and its sole effect was to leave us with a deep-rooted habit of smoking which we considered one of the prerequisities of undercover work. We wore sunglasses too to hide our manly tears when we celebrated the end of secondary school and made our farewells and promises to one another.

We each went our own way after that. He moved to Jerusalem to complete his studies at the Arab College. He then came back to our town and got a job as an English teacher in the local secondary school, where he still works to this day. Since the establishment of the State of Israel, I have had no contact with him whatsoever. He would even avoid saying hello if ever we happened to meet in the street. This estrangement pained me at first, till I got used to it and I put him out of my life altogether as soon as I realized that he was that kind of person; just like a woman before she gets married, she never puts down a novel until she finds another, but when she finds a husband she never reads anything again, not even the newspaper clippings in the lavatory.

Our friend, with whom I would exalt the conquests of Khalid Ibn al-Walid, the elegies of al-Mutanabbi, the atheistics of Abu al-Alaa and Arabism, had married his job.* What else could he do if he were to keep hold of it under Israel? For it is necessary that one cuts all ties with any friend or relative, even if it is one's own brother, the son of one's own mother and father, if he is an agitator against the state.

---

* Ibn al-Walid is an Arab military hero of the early Islamic conquests; al-Mutanabbi and Abu al-Alaa (al-Maari) are classical Arab poets.

Then, one night after the Six Day War, he suddenly knocked on my door, sat down with me after an estrangement of twenty years and said, 'Listen till the end . . .'

What was it that had put this lion into his heart and made him dare to visit me? Mister M continued where he had left off.

'With the hairs that fell to my first razor blade, Sidney Carton vanished from my album of heroes, but the title of Dickens's novel, *A Tale of Two Cities*, has continued to haunt and enchant me and colour my taste all these long years. Its influence appeared in ways which confused me at first, but then I succumbed to it. I even began to carry it around, harbouring some affection for it, treasuring it like a person with a charm which his mother hung around his neck when he was a child.

'It was not long after these strange effects began that I started to write *A Tale of Two Cities* of my own, about two cities from our country, Haifa and Nazareth. As soon as I wrote the first chapter, the story ended; so I put it aside. Then I decided to specialize in two subjects, English and Law, but nothing came of it. I took up writing poetry in English and Arabic but I managed to write nothing in either language. It saddens me that I only had one son when I really wanted two. Just ask your own boy whom I teach in the secondary school and he'll tell you how I always set them two books to read, two poets to memorize, two literatures to compare and two hours for the exam. And there are other things in my life, no need to mention them now, that confirm the hold of that duality, that bewitching title *A Tale of Two Cities*, over my taste and my mind. But surely you must have noticed that when we were friends in our youth. Have you forgotten how you gave me the nickname "the man with two chins"?'

'You were huge, with really chubby cheeks . . .'

'No. I was just like you with one chin. You called me that because I loved to repeat the phrase, "I do not mind a bearded chin or a powdered chin." Two chins, a man's chin

177

and a woman's chin, two, *A Tale of Two Cities.* This is the duality, the charm I have worn around my neck since I was a child.'

This old friend of mine is a tidy person, in attire and in speech. He is extravagant in his conversation but without affectation, so I let him ramble on as I used to in the past, especially since I was so amazed by his sudden appearance. In my case I wanted to ascertain the purpose of his visit. I believe that I had begun to understand and I said to myself that one of two things had happened: either the war had stirred something in his conscience and made him, after twenty years, come and explain the break in relations by this duality; or someone had sent him to me for something or other, and he wanted to revive our friendship by talking about this enchanting duality. I was on my guard and I looked forward to the end of his monologue.

He said, 'That's why I wasn't too surprised when we drove up the winding road of al-Laban Heights for the first time after the June War, on our way from Nablus to Ramallah.

'I let out a great grasp as we took the first bend and my tongue shook as I held the steering wheel. I shouted to my colleagues who were with me in the car. For twenty years I've been dreaming of this winding road. This hill hasn't been out of my mind for a single day. I can remember every bend. There are four; count them. And those mountains, stretching up, guarding the green plain. There are ten; count them. This pure air. This fragrance I know. I'm breathing in an aroma that's been with me all my life. This place is my place!'

I understood . . . at last I understood why the poor man had come to me after a break of twenty years. My childhood friend! How cruel time had been to us! I'm sorry I ever doubted you. I almost stood up to embrace him but he didn't give me a chance.

Mister M did not pause in his monologue. 'My friends

agreed, after I had insisted, to let me stop the car at the last bend, the fourth. They got out with me so that we could inhale that air and feast our eyes on the view of the mountains and the sheltered plain. Almond trees covered the plain and the hillsides. They really should have called the place Almond Bends. Something inside me told me to prostrate myself; something in my eyes was melting into tears. I felt like someone beholding a wonderful spectacle unfolding right in front of his eyes, as if I was reliving the years of my youth, in the haunts of my youth, not just seeing them but living them, breathing their air, feeling the blood of youthfulness, with the smell of fresh bread and dried figs, coursing through my veins.

'But my colleagues did not give me enough time and they soon brought me down from the heights of those winding roads to the lowliness of my reality. One of them wanted us to continue on our way immediately because our permits did not allow us to stop at al-Laban Heights, while another mocked my memories of the place by reminding me how, twenty years before, I had stopped to relieve myself on one of the bends. There was other banter too of the kind we teachers indulge in when we are away from our students and our wives.

'I kept on brooding upon this astonishing incident all the way to Ramallah, on to Jerusalem and then Bethlehem and during the return journey. I pleaded with my memory to retrieve what it was that happened to me during my youth, in that same spot, that had made me stand there, spellbound, never wanting to leave it, ever.

'But it was no use and when we reached the place on the way back we drove by without stopping. One of my colleagues noticed my distress. He put his hand on my shoulder to console me and said, "It looks like the heights at al-'Abhariya on the road from Nazareth to Haifa. Maybe you've got them mixed up."

'His words lifted a huge weight off my mind. For about twenty years I have been going to Haifa twice a week to give extra lessons in a secondary school and I used to pass by al-'Abhariya Heights on the way there and back. My colleague had convinced me with his simple explanation, even though I knew the two places bore no resemblance to one another whatsoever, because I am well aware of my own secret and my weak spot for *A Tale of Two Cities*. There was no doubt that al-'Abhariya Heights had always been linked in my imagination with al-Laban Heights. I accepted the explanation and felt much relieved.'

How strange man is! Does he really slaughter in his memory those things which he cannot bear to recollect? I used to think that people with no consciences developed hearts of stone so that they wouldn't feel guilt. But that's not the case. If a person is unable to kill his conscience he kills his memory! So, why had he come to tell me this story?

My old friend went on, 'You may recall that I had a number of friends and acquaintances in the West Bank, from schooldays and from later on: teachers, lawyers, doctors, businessmen, politicians, one minister and would-be ministers. I have visited them all and we have rekindled former memories and renewed former friendships. They have become once again, as they were twenty years ago, a very dear part of my life. Not a week goes by without me visiting one of them or one of them visiting me. I thought in the past that they had forgotten me or were ashamed of me and had cut me off the tree of their lives as one prunes a dead branch so that the tree can grow and burst into leaf.'

'But we are a branch that life has sprouted . . .'

'Right. At first I would visit them hesitatingly, unsure of how they would receive me but then I would find an unexpected nostalgia for old friendship and a pride in it. I found that they had kept up to date with our news; they had picked it up from the beaks of birds. And I found also that they hold us in greater esteem than we hold ourselves. I had wanted to hide from them my twenty-year withdrawal into my shell; but it turned out that they knew and understood perfectly. They saw me differently than I saw myself. They thought highly of me, and I lived up to it. They lifted me up and I stood tall, and my head rose above the blows.

'That's why I told you that they had become such a valuable part of my life . . . the life you used to know twenty years ago.'

'Did you visit me openly tonight, with you so tall?'

'Is there any way I can visit you other than openly?'

'But is that why you visited me?'

'No. There is something worrying me, keeps me awake at night. I've told you already that the feeling of surprise engendered by the winding road of al-Laban Heights was short-lived. I had put it down to the charm which had clung to me all my life, to the duality of my thought process and my logic and to my constant exposure to a similar group of hills at al-'Abhariya.

'I've driven up and down the winding road at al-Laban dozens of times since then and if ever that strange painful longing comes over me, I have an immediate explanation to relieve my conscience. That was until one day last February. I was with my wife and son on our way back from visiting some friends in Old Jerusalem. It was noon as we began to wind our way down the road at al-Laban. The almond blossoms were opening, red and white embracing in spring rapture, and all ten hills were dancing.'

'What language did you compose this ode in?'

'The language of my eyes and my heart. And you will listen to me until I finish speaking.

'My wife insisted we stop the car to pick some sprigs from an ancient almond tree which I believe had been there also in the old days. We got out and picked four sprigs. They smiled at us and we smiled back at them.

'And when my wife asked, "Is it true that if you plant an

almond sprig in the soil a tree grows?" my heart sank and I began to remember.

'Do you remember, when we were still young, we had a friend. He fell in love with a girl from Jersualem or Bethlehem, somewhere like that, and we loved this love.'

'We all fell in love, and we loved his love.'

'In fact our friend's love was more beautiful than ours. There was a story to it. We were on a trip. We stopped by that tree at the bottom of al-Laban Heights. There was a house there with chickens and cows. The house is still standing but I no longer see any chickens or cows. We asked the occupants for water. Then all of a sudden a group of girls turned up, on a trip from Jerusalem. They picked branches of almond blossom. Our friend's girl-friend was one of them. They met and she gave him a sprig full of blossoms. Were you with us?'

'What happened next?'

'I remember a beautiful story about it. I don't know how I came to hear about it, but his girlfriend broke off two sprigs from the branch. One she gave to him, the other she kept for herself. They made a pact that each one would keep their sprig and that they would meet again the following spring, when the almond trees blossom, and he would come with his family to ask her hand in marriage. What was the end of their beautiful story?'

'Why are you so interested in them?'

'I don't know. I just feel a really strong impulse pushing me to revive all my old friendships. It is as if I want to bind my present to my past so that they will never again become undone. It was a past overflowing with hope. It embraced the world and all that was in it and it was pure and open like a child's eyes. I feel today as if I want to grab its threads and extricate myself from this present. Do you think that I am actually drowning, holding on to threads of air?'

'Search me!'

'Ever since the June War I've been making my troubled

rounds in search of old friends and every time I meet one of them I get an even greater desire to meet others. You see, since I remembered the story of that friend of ours I've been searching for him, always on the lookout. None of my old friends recalls his story. It's an obsession that has got me in trouble more than once for I can hardly meet one of those old friends without insisting he tells me how he met his wife.

'And now there is no one left from the days of our youth except you to ask about this friend of ours. That's why I came. Do you remember him? It would put my mind at rest.'

'You were always a strange one, my friend, but tonight you're stranger than ever. Why are you so obsessed with a side issue?'

'You say a side issue! I realize now that I had never withdrawn into my shell, or curled up except when I cut my links with the past. What is this past? The past isn't a time. The past is you and so-and-so and so-and-so and all the friends. It's like we drew the picture of this past and each one of us coloured it with his own special colour until it emerged, an image of shining youth, to embrace everything in the whole world. I will never regain my links with this past until the parts of the picture are complete with all their colours. I see this friend of ours, with his beautiful love, I see him as the smile in this picture. What past remains without him? What would remain of *La Gioconda* if her smile were wiped away? It is his story; whether it ended joyfully in the return of the lover to his beloved or sadly in everlasting separation, his story I see as the most truthful expression of the springtime of our past. I want this past to return like the spring returns after every winter.'

'I see you've returned to the tale of the two cities, the two sprigs, the lover and his beloved, the happy ending and the sad ending. But life is not lines moving along independently of one another. It is lines intertwining.

Why couldn't it be that your imagination, awakened by a spring-like nostalgia for lofty mountains, conceived the whole story?'

'Certainly my imagination has awakened and I never want it to sleep again. That's why I am looking for our friend. Am I to presume that you don't remember him?'

'Let me think about it. If I do remember him, I'll let you know.'

Mister M left more troubled than I had ever seen him in my life, and I remained where I was, more troubled than I had ever been in mine. For a few minutes after his departure I had to restrain myself forcibly from running after him and shaking his memory back to life.

But, can I bring back the dead?

How could I not remember the beautiful love story whose hero Mister M was so anxious to remember? And how many times had I asked myself: How can a person kill in his heart a love like that?

After the June War, I had visited the good and loyal woman in Jerusalem or Bethlehem – or somewhere like that, as Mister M would say. She showed me the withered almond branch which she still kept and which almost kindled red and white as she told me its story. She told me that he had visited her with some of his teaching colleagues. He was in an excellent mood and had talked all the time. She took them into her office to look at the books and artefacts she had collected and he noticed the withered almond branch. He asked her about it and she told him that the almond blossoms in February. He changed the subject to apricots and his apricot harvest. She was extremely surprised. But now, after Mister M has visited me and told me his tale, I understand everything.

I am convinced that Mister M is sincere in his forgetfulness and is sincere in his anxiety to remember. By some strange subconscious desire he has truly forgotten that he himself is the hero of the beautiful love story, and that it was his smile that shone on our youth.

Is it my duty to remind him, to put his mind at rest as he asked? And why should I put his mind at rest? And anyway, am I really going to put his mind at rest?

If he has really stood tall, like he told me, then he should manage to get hold of this story and read it. I wonder if then he will remember, re-establish ties with his past and extricate himself from his present?

At last the almond blossomed and we met. Spring was smiling and fate absolutely roaring with laughter.

Translated by Anthony Calderbank

A Summons

Ahmed Omar Shaheen

The messenger said, 'Your grandmother summons you to make an end of your estrangement.'

Joyfully, I hurried off. He led me to a place thick with trees and cabins all in a row, with wire mesh windows, a place where humans and animals live as neighbours.

He pointed to an old woman asleep on a bed, and left.

I pushed back the branches and went in. As far as I could remember, it was she. Beside her was a woman who seemed to be her servant and who handed me a glowing coal.

She whispered, 'Hold this glowing coal.'

I contemplate asking my grandmother about her relatives to make sure she is really my grandmother.

The woman repeats, 'Hold this glowing coal, so that we can be absolutely certain that you are her awaited relative.'

I was afraid, but the urge for a reunion and an end to the estrangement made me hold and press upon it.

I looked at my grandmother's face, and between our two faces drifted the faces of our relatives. My eyes welled up with tears.

I thought that she would embrace and kiss me, that we would weep together and live with each other.

Instead, she hit the wall with her hand and said to the woman, 'You bring a stranger to trifle with me!'
And she turned her face to the wall.

Translated by Nur Elmessiri

With Both of His Hands

Ghassan Kanafani

The old man opened the door of the room. It groaned, letting out a tired, weary sound. His small shadow was cast by the light of the room across the alley's cobblestones. It was a quiet moonlit night. He stopped to feel his way across the doorstep with his thick cane and then, breathing heavily, slipped out, taking small steps, and headed towards the neighbour's garden.

This was the first time he had left his bare room in four years. He had nearly forgotten how anyone could walk without falling over. But now he could no longer afford such forbearance. Perhaps he had spent his life in ignorance and misery; but he had finally learned a lesson, small and simple, but nevertheless very essential. If you want to get anything, you have to grab at it with both of your hands.

In any case, he does not want anything grand now. Life is almost over and this heart has little enough energy for beating. But he wants simply to get that small thing he has been thinking of for the last four weeks. And if anyone tries to lend a helping hand, he will never get that small thing. If he wants it, he has to take it himself. He has to grab it with both of his hands.

His knees shook like a branch broken in the middle as he swayed in the dark, silent alley. And when, shortly, he stopped to get his breath, an angry sentence slipped from his lips, 'You senile old man!' He realized at that moment that this little sentence had repeated itself, tirelessly and incessantly, on his tongue for the last four years. And in spite of the passing of time, it had lost none of its meaning or significance or insidiousness. It still sent a blazing rage through his feeble bones, as if he were hearing it for the first time, as if his first-born, his son, standing in the middle of the room, hands in pockets, eyeing his father coldly, was saying it now, at this very moment.

He shook his cane angrily and narrowed his eyes in order to see clearly, but he could not take a single step. Anger had so filled his breast that it blocked his throat. You senile old man! He lost his bearings for a moment and leaned on a nearby tree trunk ... senile old man! But not now ... I have finally learned this useful small lesson: if you want something, grab it with both hands ... No, I won't ever again stand humiliated in front of you, Khairy.

Again, he saw the incident in its entirety. It was four years ago. Khairy had come to tell him that he could not live with him, but that he would give him a room somewhere and a maid who would come for an hour every two days to see to his laundry and food ... At that moment, he knew that he had lost everything in the world. Sad, paralysed, rage blazed inside him, sad, paralysed. He looked around, not knowing why he did not say anything but instead made for Khairy standing in the middle of the room, hands in pockets, and fell to his knees before him and tried to kiss his hand. But Khairy pulled his hand away violently, stepped back and yelled at the top of his voice, 'You? You senile old man!'

Me, a senile old man! A senile old man because I wanted to tell you that life is not just a room, a maid, clothes and food. Am I a senile old man because I loved you, because I humbled myself at your feet ... because I asked you, begged you, pleaded with you to give me what I want, because I did not grab what I wanted with both hands ...

'You senile old man!' He said it once again, dragging his

feet across the sand in the garden. And once again it sent a bitter, deadly anger through his blood. But he found solace when he began to think once more of how this time he would get what he wanted and without asking anyone for it. He could have asked the maid, or his neighbour, or any little boy walking down the road in the morning to go to that spot in the garden and bring him the kitten. Except he insisted on doing this himself. He had promised himself not to ask anyone for anything. He cannot bear a new disappointment, not even a minor one . . .

In the corner of the garden, he could make out the black cat lying by the wall. She lifted her head and peered at him through two bright eyes. He hung his cane on his arm, took a small bag out of his pocket and bent over to look for her kittens. Two of them were sleeping beside her with closed eyes and little tails. Not far from her was the third kitten lying with its eyes wide open, its tail hitting the garden dust in regular beats. 'That's the one,' the old man said to himself. He came closer and lifted it. It was the size of his palm, its fur, black like the night, its eyes, as green as spring. He dropped it slowly into the bag. The mother meowed in distress and sprang, erect, on to her agile limbs. He paid no attention, wrapped the upper part of the bag around his wrist and turned back, dragging himself away slowly. The mother followed for a few steps, then stopped, then followed him, meowing intermittently. He threw her a quick glance and repeated to himself, 'If you want something, grab it with both of your hands.'

He shook with excitement as he opened the door to his bare room. It groaned, letting out a tired, weary sound. He searched with his eyes for his big white cat and found him stretched out under the table. 'We'll see what will happen now . . .' he thought with relish. He dropped the bag on the floor and the black kitten came out slowly and stood shaking, looking around. The big white cat lifted his head and looked for a moment. He then walked over slowly, lazily, to the kitten, circled round him twice, sniffed from a distance, reached his paw out to feel his head and then went back to his spot under the table . . .

The old man felt slightly disappointed but pretended not to care and went back to his bed without for a moment ceasing to observe the two cats. Except nothing happened for an hour. Just when the old man was about to nod off, he heard a strange sound in the room and opened his eyes thoughtfully. He directed his eyes to where the bag was but did not find the black kitten. He pulled himself out of bed and looked under the table . . . The big white cat was lying on its side while the black kitten had nuzzled its head in, looking voraciously for a nipple from which to feed.

'He's hungry,' the old man said out loud. When he left his bed to look for something with which to feed the black kitten, an idea suddenly occurred to him, immediately filling him with a real joy. 'No, I won't feed him. And let's see what will happen. . .'

The old man went back to his bed and sat on its edge rubbing his hands together. The black kitten was still trying its best to find a nipple that would give him milk on the white cat's belly. But, after a few moments, the white cat jumped up on the table and lay on top of it while the other one meowed, looking up, miserable at not being able to follow.

'You poor little kitten,' the old man said out loud. 'You don't know that this isn't your mother. Or that this is a male cat that cannot give you anything . . .'

He shook his head bitterly and continued to address the black kitten, 'I know that you're hungry and that you don't eat except what your mother feeds you . . . But that's life, you poor little thing . . . People lose their mothers and fathers, and mothers and fathers lose their children. And every creature has to fend for itself . . .'

But the kitten continued its distressed, plaintive meowing. The other cat had come close to the edge of the

191

table and was looking down with wide-open eyes at the black creature which, in spite of its small size, was making its strange demand loudly.

In spite of all the noise made by the kitten, the old man lay down in his bed, pleased with the life that had suddenly sprung up in the bare room. The incessant shrill meowing did not prevent the old man from falling asleep. When he woke up at dawn, he leaned on his pillow and looked around the room for the two cats and eventually spotted them near the doorstep: the big white cat lying on its side letting the little black creature suck ravenously at its breast hairs, making the sounds of a suckling baby.

He got out of his bed, bent over the two cats and said in a hoarse voice, 'In spite of this, poor little one, you will not slake your thirst . . .' At this, the white cat lifted its head and gazed at the old man with imploring eyes, then shut them again in surrender. The old man, as if knowing what the cat wanted, bent over again and went on speaking to him in a hoarse voice, 'I know that you're not happy with me . . . But I am not happy about anything . . . It's true I took him away from his mother's bosom, but I too was kicked out of my son's arms . . . Khairy, for whom I had given away my very eyes . . . You must understand this, big white cat . . . You've lived with me for four years in this mad loneliness . . .'

But the cat did not open its eyes again. So the old man merely shook his head stubbornly and turned around to get back into his bed. Before he lay down, he wondered out loud, 'For how long will this go on? There must come a moment . . .' There was nothing to prevent him from falling asleep once again.

It was only when the door opened that he remembered that today was the day the maid came. So he buried his head under the quilt as usual. He hated this stern maid and refused to engage in conversation with her, enduring her incecssant chatter with as much patience as he could muster . . . But this time she came horribly close to his bed.

He heard the sound of her shoes stepping towards him and then stop. Then he heard her gasp as she lifted the quilt up away from his head. He looked at her staring at him with terrified eyes. She pointed to the doorstep and screamed, 'Look over there!'

The old man sat up slowly in bed and let his gaze fall on the doorstep. At first he couldn't believe his eyes. But the scene was clear and real: The black kitten was still lying there; it had sunk its tiny fangs into the white cat's breast as it lay stretched out in an acquiescent silence, its deep eyes open in consent. The red glistening blood flowed down through the bright white hair as the suckling kitten sucked loud and ravenously.

Translated by Nur Elmessiri

The Madman's Awakening

Hassan Hemeid

They're waking me now! What happened? Did my people return to their neighbourhood? And did the first funeral begin? I don't know. All that I know is that they're waking me.

One of them is poking my shoulder. I feel pain and don't complain. I ask him to stop his poking as I don't wish to rise. My face is pale and my feet are leaden weights and I choke on my words. Still, he doesn't stop poking.

The flesh on my shoulder disintegrates. My pain increases and becomes sharper. My body continues to be dead. It does not pull itself up or respond to the poker's calls. It remains stretched out on the ground. The poker notices that the flesh of my shoulder is strewn about and so he pokes my other shoulder sharply. I do not rise, as if all strength has left me or perhaps my ability to feel pain has died.

We had agreed that, after I went down into my grave and stretched out in it, they would not wake me up unless my people returned to their home and the first funeral came to the camp. I long to see a funeral procession and to hear the songs, the rejoicing and the sound of shots being fired.* For a long time, I have yearned to see funeral

---

*Firing in the air is traditionally an expression of rejoicing at occasions such as weddings.

194

processions returning once more to the camp, after having ceased, after having been stopped by them.

And now they are waking me! When they received me in my grave, my new home, and after the people of the camp had returned, they said to me, 'We are two angels from God. Do you know us?'

I said, 'I know you well.'

'And we know you well, too,' they said. 'You are the madman of the camp, outcast by night and by day, and your name is Taja Abu Hilal. The boys of the camp used to lift the hem of your *qumbaz* to see your nudity and you would scold them. The grown-ups would laugh and the women would cheer. We know of the darkness of your nights and your indifference about the existence or non-existence of God. We know of your adventures and of your attempts to get closer, in the night, to the camp's madwoman Um Jaraab. And we know, also, many things.'

Then they were silent. When the silence had all but engulfed them, fearlessly I asked them, 'And do you know about my love?'

'Yes,' they said.

I didn't ask them about it for they are angels from God who know many things. They must know about my love. So I kept quiet and hid my head under a black stone which the people from the camp had placed under my head. But the two angels lifted the stone away from my head and said affectionately and lovingly (I do not know why they were so affectionate to me and so loving), 'We will now let you sleep in peace. We will not make you suffer or judge you today. Life has worn you out a lot. Your daily bread was sorrow as was your waking and your sleeping. We will let you sleep in peace, but dare not slip, during your waking state, into your neighbours' graves. And now we will leave you. So, before you sleep, tell us if you have a question, a wish or an aim for us to realize for you before we leave.'

Pleading, begging, deferential, I said to them, 'I want to

be fully awake when my people return and to be able to see the first funeral procession pass once more through the camp alleys, accompanied by the hymns and ululations of joy, surrounded by the old and the young, covered by the remains of rice and lentil grains and salt.'

They nodded their consent and left me.

I fell asleep at once and did not wake till now, now that both – or perhaps it's just one of them – are waking me. I opened my eyes and let some strength flow through my body. I leaned on one of the walls of the grave and sat up. I looked around me and found them sitting in the dark looking at me. I asked them joyfully, 'Did they return to their home and has the first funeral begun?'

They did not speak.

The situation worried me and my thoughts became confused. 'Perhaps Um Jaraab died and the camp was left without a lunatic,' I said to myself. 'Perhaps the people of the camp are surrounding me now, trying to open my grave to put her inside.' So I rejoiced and prepared to receive her. Inside this grave, we will meet again and be as one, far from the stares and suspicious whispers. I will tell her why I went mad and she will do the same. Little by little, she and I together will come back to our senses. I waited for her arrival without asking the two angels whether or not I had guessed right. I looked at them and found them tongue-tied. I waited for a long time but my grave did not open. I thought that perhaps the Day of Judgment had come, that perhaps, in this waking state, I was waiting for my turn to be resurrected and raised from the dead, to come out from under the roof of my grave. But my waiting seemed to have been very long.

So I asked the two angels again what had happened but they did not answer my question. I said to myself, 'Perhaps I've been lying in this grave for a long time and the people from the camp have gone, through many funerals, back home, have cultivated their land and have held their weddings over there beyond the river. Perhaps they took no notice of my presence to bid me farewell and, saying that I was a madman who could not understand the meaning of a farewell or of a greeting, they left. Or perhaps I didn't see any of them as they left because the two angels were slow to wake me up. But no, I can hear a strange sound outside. I hear a cacophony of screaming and crying of young and old. I hear the voice of Zahrat al-Issa, the widow of Abu Ismail who died a martyr in South Lebanon. (I remember very well the day they brought his corpse to the camp. It was covered by the national flag and was carried in a grey Land Rover. On that day, all the people of the camp came out in a procession to cheer Abu Ismail to his grave. On that day I sang for him. I sang for him and for all the sons and daughters of the camp. I sang my usual song, 'Green, O martyr, green, green.')

I hear Zahrat al-Issa saying, 'Where do we go?'

Her question puzzles me and fills me with amazement. Maybe she's lost her mind and doesn't know where she's going any more. Very strange! Maybe her little children, after they grew up, followed in their father's footsteps and died as martyrs, leaving her lonely and helpless. Maybe it is because of her loneliness that the world has become too small for her. But I hear her adding, 'And the little ones, where do I take them?'

Good heavens! Maybe I haven't been lying down for such a long time. Zahrat al-Issa's children are still children and haven't yet joined their father. But why are these two angels waking me up now if the people of the camp have not returned home and the first funeral has not yet begun?

I try to ask them again, mustering up the energy to do so, but the voice of Rashad al-Badeer, one of the strong revolutionary fighters who lives in the western alley of the camp, screams (his screaming paralyses my question and clots it in the cavity of my mouth), 'There is neither might nor power but in Him who has power.'

And, wringing his hands in despair, he stopped speaking.

I was taken aback and confused. I mumbled to myself, 'If Rashad al-Badeer says, "There is neither might nor power but in Him who has power," then what should the others say? The calamity must be enormous. What is it that has happened?'

I threw myself at the two angels, touching them and especially their beards with my two hands in supplication, begging them to tell me what had happened. But they remained silent, motionless and hard. The sounds outside became louder and spread out. I hear the sound of footsteps approaching me. Near my grave, they almost disappear and then, shunning it, they head towards another.

I listen carefully; without any doubt, it's the sound of footsteps, of many feet racing through the paths of the cemetery. I rejoice. It must be that they intend to return to our homes and so one of them will have to stand near my grave and take leave of me. For I am not greedy; one is enough for me, one who says, 'Farewell, Abu Hilal,' and leaves. I do not ask for more than this.

I listen more carefully. I hear voices rising near me, very close to me, voices choking on bitterness, pain and disappointment. I hear them very clearly. A voice says, 'Goodbye, mother, they've deported us.'

I know this voice: it's the voice of Awda al-Fayyad (the man who repairs the primus stoves) taking leave of his mother. He says to her, 'They've deported us.'

Puzzled, I wonder who has deported him but have no answer. Another voice reaches me, 'Farewell, Abu Yassin. I'll take good care of the children.' It's the voice of Dindy al-Abboud. Strange! Is she still alive? And this is the voice of Mohamed al-Faraj, taking leave of his father: 'Oh, father, I fear I will not come back . . . goodbye.'

The hoarseness of his voice pains me. I listen carefully

to hear the voice of the schoolteacher. It reaches me, faint and broken, as he takes leave of three of his pupils. An explosive device blew up their bodies near the school fence where they were playing.

'I'm sorry, my children,' he says to them. 'I was wrong when I told you that the camp would remain, even after our return to our land and till the Day of Judgment, to tell the coming generations that we had once been exiled in it.'

I hear him add, 'I remember telling you that our camps would later become museums of our struggle, to be visited. But now, what we had never dreamed of has come to pass: the camp is passing away and will not remain. Farewell.' I hear the sound of his footsteps growing fainter.

Bitterly, I wonder, 'What has happened? Why is the camp passing away?'

I ask the two angels, but they do not answer.

My eyes roam about the grave. I look for a crack or an opening which would connect me to the outside world so that I can see what is happening in the camp. I find a dry plant root hanging down into my grave. I pull the root downwards, tear it out and, from where I lie, I join the world through the light creeping in to me through the hole. Daylight must be streaming through the camp. I peer through the hole, see nothing but the overcast face of the sky and the darkness thickening over the horizon. I reach for the hole and, with my bony fingers, widen it.

As soon as the task was accomplished, I got up, and tried to get out through it. I got my head out and the upper half of my body. And when I had nearly left the grave, the two angels gripped my feet and held my body back. I begged them and pleaded with them to let me step out for just a few moments to find out what was happening in the camp and then return to my grave and my sleep. But they did not agree. I grumbled a lot while glancing around me to see what was happening. And I saw.

I saw the women wailing and the men at a loss, the forlorn glances, the children whispering and spitting.* I saw many tin sheets and kitchen tiles and tin sheets crumpled up into balls, and near them stood two men with a bunch of children. The first man I know very well: it's Hassan al-Khumayis. I hear him saying to the other man (whom I don't know at all and who is stuffed in elegant bright clothes), 'I won't sell it, Effendi. I'll take it with me to another place and set it up and, beneath its roof, I'll toast the bread, me and my children. I won't sell it, never.'

As he walked away, outpacing him, the Effendi said, 'You'll regret it.'

I also saw strange machines, yellow, like the locusts of the Negev Desert near the sea. The machines were guarded by men wearing helmets the colour I hate and which I hate to mention by name because of all that I saw. They have heavy black cudgels in their hands. Some of them have stars on their shoulders. I saw the machines tearing down the alleys and houses of the camp, indifferent to the anger of the whose pictures martyrs supported the walls. I saw them scatter the tin sheets and raze the houses to the ground.

I couldn't bear to watch this scene, wondering, 'Why is this happening?'

I meant to return to the depths of the grave, but instead, I infused the body with resolution and the head with pride, wishing to charge into the machines, towards those guarding them, to say to them, 'This cannot be! You're erasing the traces of the steps we took in our funerals, erasing the decoration on our walls which we entrusted with our cries, calamities and hopes. Stop this.'

But I didn't charge at them; I didn't say anything to them; I didn't get to know the reason for what had

---

*Spitting is at times an expression of disgust, sometimes mixed, as here, with fury

happened; no, after the two angels had pulled me into it, I was forced back down into my grave. They laid me out and closed up the hole with the same root and with the dust that I had dug up. They then recited something in their own tongue upon me. I began to fall asleep slowly to the sound of the machines sweeping the camp and its alleys away, closing my ears, indifferent to the cacophony of the screams, mumbles and whispers of the people of the camp. Compelled, I went back to dwelling in my sleep. But I did not fall asleep.

Translated by Magda Amin

Four Colours

Ahmed Omar Shaheen

I hear voices from the distance, urging me to run. I run and
run, the bullets whizzing all around me. I pant, as if I have
covered league upon league. I am surprised by a band of
musicians carrying their instruments who overtake me.
They have long beards. Their hair shows thick beneath
their hats. Their clothes do not match. They appear to be
the fanatical rabbis who live in the settlement nearby.

'What has brought these people to the village today?' I
asked myself. A foreboding of evil stole upon me. I looked
for my sling – but could not find it. My hand felt for the
dagger that I hide under my clothes but found no trace of
it. The musicians began to play and the whole street rang
with music.

Heads leaned out of windows and over balconies and
little boys and girls came out of the houses to stand on the
pavements and watch. I changed my mind and instead of
returning home, decided to follow them.

Crowds gathered. I thought it would turn into a large
demonstration, but the children were not ready, as was
their wont, with stones. What also surprised me was the
tune they were playing. It was the music of 'My Homeland, My Homeland'.

'Is it possible,' I said to myself, 'for settlers to play the
Palestinian national anthem? It must be a band from a
neighbouring village.'

I edged up to the bandleader to ask him. He smiled and, raising his hat in a salute, held it towards me. Meanwhile, the band had begun playing 'O my Flag, O Flag'. I took out all the money I had and put it in the hat.

He took the money out and looked at it, his face clouding over with sorrow.

'Do you want to bring a curse upon us,' he asked, 'by giving us forged money?'

'Forged? These are new shekels!' I replied in astonishment.

'Are you making fun of me? This money is no longer in use. You know . . . since . . .'

He raised his head and pointed at the sky. Following the direction of his hand, I was astounded to see Palestinian flags fluttering over every building. I began to notice things that, throughout my walk behind them, had escaped my attention.

I left him as he was saying, 'We're trying to earn our bread peacefully. Please don't make fun of us.'

It was a sunny spring morning. The fountains in the square were spouting water heavenwards, reflecting, as the sunbeams caught it, the colours of the rainbow. Children were playing and making merry. I ran towards them. Even though I did not know them, they cheered when they saw me. Never before had my village been this beautiful. I felt joyful as they carried me and raised me upwards. I rose with the water gushing sky high, like a butterfly bedewed with drizzle, embracing the tune, the flowers and the fragrance, and shrouded in a rainbow of four colours.

Translated by Sahar Hamouda

The Procession

Mahmoud al-Rimawi

No sooner had he come out from prayers than we, his comrades, came forward and carried him on our palms and shoulders, our heads lifted, our hearts bowed and filled with anger and grief. With steady, regular steps we began to cut our path through the stunned crowds. We covered a short distance and no sooner had we arrived at the main road than we each felt the coffin shake with a slow tremulous movement. Because this was the first time I had ever had the privilege of performing such a duty, I did not realize at once what was happening. I glanced at the comrade next to me so that he could help me, only to find him sending me ambiguous looks. And I saw that the two comrades at the front were doing the same. Each of us looked questioningly, in a cautious, reserved way, for the loftiness of the situation did not permit more than that or allow otherwise.

Suffocated, we slowly continued with our procession as if – except for our having lost a dear brother forever – nothing unusual had happened. With sore hearts and uncollected thoughts, we carried him on our palms and shoulders on a wooden carrier – he whom the wide world was not wide enough to hold. (If only the dead would take charge of himself, would leave a letter and a will and would hurry, before his death, to his grave and sort himself out there and sleep! Is that not more dignified than being laid on a wooden stretcher and being carried on the shoulders of others?)

The coffin was heavy. Perhaps it was a bit heavier on my side. But grief was more intense and more bitter in the throat and in the heart of hearts. You were snatched from us in a night of bullets. We were deprived, though we hadn't prepared ourselves for this, of completing the circle of friendship.

The coffin stirred once more. It stirred and the earth beneath us stirred; the banners stirred; and the horizon.

'Steady now, boys,' one of the two comrades at the front said in a low voice, careful that his words would not reach ears other than ours. But it was not that we lacked steadiness, it was that our brother in the coffin had moved. And why shouldn't he move? Who would content himself with lying on a rectangular wooden board and with remaining there, motionless? But how could we be sure about what had happened? How?... Should we put the coffin down in the middle of the road and unwrap the corpse and examine it? We would be raving mad to do that. And his close relatives would be suspicious. We were one family, uncles and brothers in real suffering and in dreams.

Some kind mourners nearby noticed our trembling forearms, faltering steps, pallid faces and wandering glances. Except for the movement in the coffin, they noticed everything and promptly came forward to take our place. They also wanted to participate in honouring the dear departed one. I asked the man who had come forward to replace me not to deprive me of this duty because of the special relationship that had bound me to the departed. He was not convinced. Usually, it is the right of everyone, including strangers, to participate in whatever way they can; it is not the exclusive right of anyone in particular, not even of the kinsmen of the departed. The man finally withdrew, muttering apologetic words, asking God to have mercy on the departed.

Before we arrived, I heard a movement within the coffin. And I did not keep quiet. I raised my voice, 'There is no God but God.' The surrounding mourners repeated the prayers with me. And then I called out, and my heart rejoiced, 'God is with us.' This time, fewer mourners responded in prayer.

He moved once again. I could never remember him still, even in his sleep. Perhaps he takes death lightly. No, death is real enough. It is murder that he mocks.

He moved and then settled down. The three new ones who had replaced my comrades did not notice this. Perhaps their thoughts were directed elsewhere.

We arrived.

The grave yawned open, waiting for the one who was about to be returned to the dust: a tiny ditch, hardly big enough to collect water or to plant an olive tree. We put the coffin down amidst the hallelujahs and *Allahu akbars* and, in spite of the frantic crowding, I made sure I was standing close to him and did not budge from my place. My comrades, whose names I need not mention, since they are commoners filling the streets and houses, disappearing and appearing at any time, did the same.

The corpse, wrapped in white cloth, lay perfectly still, except for the face which I saw overflowing with dreams. I had meant to give it a loving kiss, but was too embarrassed. In situations like this, men should not get carried away. They lifted him. Three men, stern and steady, without turning around to look at anyone, lifted him and began to let him down slowly towards the bottom of the ditch. They did not leave this task to us, his devoted comrades. They put a rock under the head, a pillow of rock, and then they made ready to put another rock over the face. Son of Adam, brother, oh what a loss! They began to heap the dust on him, energetically and with enthusiasm. On the verge of sobbing out loud, I kept moving my tearful glances from the ditch to my three friends and back again, all the time afraid of being accused of slackening. As if in agreement, our quiet departing friend let them carry out the sacred routine as they wished.

Before his tall glowing frame had disappeared and before his modest, red-cheeked face vanished, my three friends and I gasped for the head had moved and the eyelids had twitched. Did the head not move? It did stir and before our dry lips could utter a word, the blind dust began to pour down as fast as fate upon his visage, burying and submerging it. A few fleeting moments and he had been buried in the earth and had gone away.

We also went away, memory clutching at his picture that had already begun to blur and fade. He watered the earth; and in the earth he was buried. We did not know how many sounds, how many movements and *intifadas* came forth from him just then and afterwards. For he parted from us and we from him. We still had to live out the rest of our days and to try to achieve, even if without him, what we had agreed upon, in the beginning.

Translated by Nur Elmessiri

Um al-Khayr

Tawfiq Fayyad

Her round face, the colour of wheat, was unfurrowed by the passing of the years. The gleaming white scarf she always draped over her silver hair, framed her peaceful features in a wondrous harmony, and fell squarely on her shoulders as if it were the pedestal supporting the head of a statue in eternal contemplation. It was impossible for anyone who had seen her to forget her head rising, like the head of a statue, above the living quarters in every ancient house of the village, above every turn in the alley. And that spring smile with her tattooed dimples – every heart had known that smile and every eye had tasted its sweetness. In her presence the old men of the village remained young and strong, and the youngsters were ever children, never growing old in her mind. In her presence time stood still, and letters ceased to circulate.

'Um al-Khayr'* was her name. That's how I, together with all the other children in our village, knew her. Everything she owned belonged to us, and everything she did generated love for the children. Even her anger. If she but laid her gracious hand upon the brow of one of our sick, he was cured, and if she touched the head of a

*Mother of Goodness

208

miscreant, he would lie in her lap like a young pigeon; our mothers would take us to her to be blessed.

And on winter days and their cruel nights, when there was no meeting with the land for our fathers or grand-fathers, then our good land and all its news would move to the house of Um al-Khayr. There the land met with the people around her fire. And despite the narrowness of its arches, the house of Um al-Khayr embraced all the land and hills of the village. Sometimes the house's love would grow around her warmth and then its arches would expand to contain our whole country . . . its summer and autumn, its winter and spring, an ever-young maiden, just like Um al-Khayr herself . . . night after night, and day after day.

The days passed and the good thing was that the goodness increased and Um al-Khayr's love grew. The people's love for her grew also, especially the love of Hassan the ploughman, he who had spent his life in her service ever since her father had entrusted him, while still a lad, to farm his land. In those days, Um al-Khayr was still a beautiful young woman and he had fallen in love with her as he loved the land itself.

People sang of their love, even after she married someone else and gave birth to her only son. Then the years passed them by and he remained true to his old silent love for her, for he had sworn an oath to himself not to love anyone else. He grew old and never married, and the people among themselves called him the hermit, for he never sat with them and his only diversion for all those long years was with the land . . . and if ever anyone happened to mention him, they would humbly lower their voice, especially in the presence of Um al-Khayr, who would look away when she heard his name and lower her head for an old lover who had adored her. No one ever dared mention her in front of Hassan, except for the shepherds who spontaneously would sing to one another songs of his love as they walked behind their sheep, passing him as he tilled his land.

Thus the days passed in our village and no one knew that one day a castastrophe would befall the house of Um al-Khayr. Of course everybody knew that the snake which had killed Um al-Khayr's husband, while she was still a young woman, had continued to live in the arches of the house . . . but since that day it had not appeared and they had come to believe that it was now on its deathbed, because it had emptied all its poison into the man's heel and also because of its age. Many years before it killed Um al-Khayr's husband, it had killed his grandfather's cattle in the front yard, and it had finished off all the pigeons in the tower. It kept on moving from place to place throughout the large house till finally it settled down between the ceiling beams. Um al-Khayr would point out to her cronies that, with the approach of summer, she had begun to hear its cackle which resembled the cluck of a hen hatching its eggs. The old men, however, assured her that this cackle that she could hear was no more than the rattle of its demise. They related various tales of aged snakes they had encountered in their long lives, or which they had heard from others, all of which confirmed that an old snake's demise sounded like the cluck of a hen hatching its eggs, and that in such a condition it would not be able to move or leave its lair until it died. They went on with such tales as these until one of them would curse the mention of the snake, because once the snake was mentioned in a conversation, the conversation would never end. Um al-Khayr, however, was unconvinced by their tales, and told them that she was ready to pull the roof down and build it again.

'Listen, you men,' she said, 'Um al-Khayr's instincts never fail. The pigeons spend all day hovering over the roof and they don't coo, and the swallows have left their nests in the arches and have flown away.'

One stifling June night, Um al-Khayr sat at the evening

meal with her son and her grandchildren before the rest of her company came. And though she saw the bubbles floating on the surface of the milk jug which hung in the western arch, she put it down to the intense heat. But no sooner had they finished their meal than the poison wiped out the lot of them . . . except for Um al-Khayr, whose cronies found her unconscious and swollen-limbed.

The noxious poison left its scourge on the body of Um al-Khayr despite all attempts by the old men to cure her, until in the end she lay like a skeleton in her bed unable to leave it. Day by day her gatherings became deserted apart from the old women who looked after her. None of us young ones even dared approach the door of her house. Our pity for her and our fear of her would lead us, despite our mothers' warnings, to the corner of the alley which led to her house. There we would wait for one of the old women to come out and we would ask for news of Um al-Khayr, if her face was still terrifying or if, as our mothers had told us, she still ate children with her long blackened teeth.

The disease caused festering sores to appear. They began to spread all over her body until in the end no one dared approach her bed any more, not even the old women who were looking after her. They were afraid they would catch the disease, for it was rumoured in the village that the sores were contagious and that in fact one of the old women had been affected . . . and had gone running hysterically through the village tearing her flesh with her nails.

Panic seized everyone in the village and some people lit fires in their houses despite the July heat because they believed that it would prevent the disease from seeping into their homes. They were waiting for her to die. Some of them fled to the olive groves on the nearby hills and stayed there with their children. It was not long before the rest joined them, despairing that she would ever be cured.

Um al-Khayr felt the gradual emptying of the village around her. Her bulging eyes met Hassan's. His old love had come back to him. He had returned to be the last one to look after her . . . She looked at him one evening. Her eternal smile appeared on her festering cheeks and fluttered around her trembling lips, ' Have all the people deserted the village, Hassan?'

Hassan smiled at her comfortingly, 'As long as Hassan is with you, Khadra, no one has deserted it.'*

'It's difficult to die, Hassan, when the people my heart loves are so far away. Do you think I'll live, Hassan, and see them around me once again?'

'Easily, Khadra . . . easily. Job almost died and got well, Khadra! After every suffering comes release . . . God is great!'

Um al-Khayr raised her little finger.

'Praise be to God. Praise be to God for His gifts and for His wisdom.'

'He deserves all praise, for good things and for bad things . . . for the difficult times and the easy times.' Their gazes embraced for a long time, and with each glance two silent tears embraced . . .

'Do you still love me, Hassan?'

'As long as the One Who granted me this love is alive, Khadra.'

'Hassan, your skin has become rough; it's time your ploughshare turned over the land, though there's no one left in this village to sing the harvest song.'

'Whatever comes from you, Khadra, is good. He who comforts you will comfort me too.'

'By God, Hassan, there's no comfort any more . . . two or three days, Hassan, and . . .'

---

* Khadra literally means 'green woman'. In the folk Arab version of the legend of Ayub (Job), Khadra is his beloved wife and cousin. She stands by him, goes to the city to sell her hair to get him medicine, but by the time she returns to him Ayub has fully and miraculously recovered.

He gently pressed his ulcerous hand upon her ulcerous lips to silence her . . .

'Of course, Um al-Khayr, you've always been strong, like a mighty sail; the storms come and go and the oaks in the mountains stand erect like young men . . . and our country's olives, Um al-Khayr, are abundant in autumn, and the olive oil overflows the casks. And in the lean months, our cattle's offspring fill our homes. As long as the mountains of this land milk the clouds in her sky and fill Um al-Khayr's jars with water, then Um al-Khayr will live and give people to drink from the jars, and the sores which have afflicted the people will be beauty marks on her cheeks and the people will be dazzled by her loveliness.'

And so Hassan consoled her with his presence, despite the sores which had begun to spread over his own body and which he treated himself with the herbs and dried roots he gathered in the mountains.

One morning Um al-Khayr awoke from her slumber and searched for him with her eyes, but he had gone out to the mountains at dawn and had not returned. The village around her was like barren casks. Not the bellow of a bull nor even the howling of a dog could she hear. She began to moan loudly for he might be outside the house and might hear her. This time she was conscious and certain of death and it pained her to die with her eyes out of her old lover's sight.

On the brink of death, her old strength was rekindled. She crawled through the door of the house towards the main gate and then on feebly through the alleys of the village, until she reached its edge overlooking the olive groves. She heard the dogs' barking coming from the groves and saw columns of smoke rising from the fires of those who had deserted her. She raised her festering body to its feet. Two tears hovered around the edges of her last smile . . . for Hassan had appeared on the road.

Her smile was the last thing that shone from her face as

Hassan stood stunned before her. Her body had begun to turn into an ancient gnarled trunk. He struck his hands together in grief.

'What a life you lived, Um al-Khayr. Not even death could get the better of you.'

Her smiling mouth let out a sigh and Hassan knelt against the trunk watering it with his bleeding sores.

The next morning, two buds appeared where her tattooed dimples had been. As the days passed they grew and sprouted branches, and each morning from their tips two tears would drop on to Hassan's sores, for she had made him sit beneath them, and each morning two of his sores would heal.

As for us youngsters, we never saw Hassan the ploughman on the mountain track where we used to meet him and ask for news of Um al-Khayr. And as we grew older, the tree that had sprouted grew bigger in the distance until its green branches contained all the houses in the village.

Translated by Anthony Calderbank

The Earth

Ahmed Omar Shaheen

I wakened to the sound of moaning. This is a dream, I thought, but the moaning was coming from inside the apartment, the cries of a woman in labour. I could not move. Then I turned on the light and looked through the keyhole. And there she was, sitting, her back supported by her hand, her legs wide apart, and between her legs two children whose umbilical cords had not yet been cut.

From behind the door I called out, 'Who are you? What brings you here?'

Lifting her head, she turned her gaze to the door. I knew her. She was my mother.

'All the pills,' I screamed, 'the pills they made you swallow. And you're pregnant.'

And then I remembered. Having resolved to open the door I retreated. I could not move forward. How could I make sense of what I saw? For had they not told me years ago that my mother was dead?

'Who are you?' The question emerged like a hiss from my mouth.

'Have you forgotten me?' she asked, 'I am your mother.'

I dared not tell her she had died.

'And my father?' I asked, 'how is he?'

She gave no answer.

'Did they not bury you six years ago?' I trembled.

'You thought so . . .'

'And all this time. Where have you been?'

'When I saw that you were in need of a child who would be of use, I came.'

'Yes,' said one of the babies, 'I will be of use to you.'

But this is insanity. A few minutes old and it speaks. My mother still capable of giving birth to a creature who speaks, like Christ, in the crib. A miracle.

'Do not be afraid,' I said. 'I will look after them, I will raise them and fulfil your expectations.'

She laughed. 'Don't worry about that,' she said. 'I brought them here not for you to look after, but to look after you.'

She disappeared and the two infants rose. I looked towards them, and we smiled.

Translated by Nur Elmessiri

VI

Dreams of Paradise Redeemed

The Tree

Rashad Abu Shawer

The wind, rain, clouds, little children and birds got together and made the following decision: although Nixon had land-mined the Gulf of Tonkin and wanted to burn everything, the leaves of the trees would remain green.

After the American B52 warplanes had continued to drop their terrible bombs over the jungles and villages of Vietnam, some targets were achieved. Tens of children were killed and the napalm burnt down thousands of trees. The roots of the trees remained firmly cemented to the earth.

A bird landed on the branch of a tree, half of which was burnt while the other half was green. The bird kept singing until the smoke around the tree trunk had cleared. Word of this reached Nixon and he made a note in his diary, 'This bird is an enemy of the free world and is on the side of the revolutionaries.' Then he issued the following order. 'All birds must be killed at once in order to guarantee my return to the presidency in the next elections.'

When the Israeli warplanes (American-made) dropped their missiles (also made in America) over the Salt mountains to burn the trees and the *fedaiyin*, some of the *fedaiyin* fell martyrs, and tens of trees burned down on the slope beyond Salt, on the way to al-Aghwar. One tree was hit by a missile and half of it was burnt (the other half remained in bloom and green). The tree did not die.

The sparrows flutter over it and then land on the half that has been burnt and made bare of green leaves. They keep singing and singing until a leaf sprouts amidst the dead branches ... then they fly away ... to return the next day ... and so on.

Translated by Karaz Mona Hamdy

The Grass

Farouk Wadi

They said that a man who loved a woman was the one who
burned the grass.

I was sad thinking of my bird who had died of hunger
that depressing morning when they came. And when I
stood before them, one of the interrogators said to me,
'Are you the one who burned the grass?'

'The grass? Me?' I spoke with real bewilderment for I
wasn't good at acting.

The men's arms stretched out. Drawn on them were
tattoos of strange faces with horns and bared teeth
breathing tongues of flame (yellow and red . . . wavy . . .
that's how I saw them). Then their fists came down, one
after the other, striking me in the face.

I staggered beneath their blows like the flame of a
lantern of a deserted monastery extinguished in the
winter . . . until I fell to the ground.

At that very moment, it occurred to me to look
carefully at my own arms. On one of them was a rose
smiling cheerfully. And on the other, letters spelling the
name of my beloved.

Translated by Anthony Calderbank

Norma and the Snowman

Yehia Yakhlaf

Nabatia was already behind them. The military administration car began to climb the slope along the narrow asphalt road which rose far up through the olive and cedar trees.

'That white mountain top is one of the Jabal al-Sheikh peaks,' the driver said. The volunteer nodded. He was about to say that he had seen it years ago from the other side, but did not speak. The car darted through one of the villages. He could not read the sign. The young men in the back seat smoked, then smoked some more and went on smoking.

This looks like our village, Bourin, he thought to himself. The houses, the people, the cactus trees and the calf-meat hanging on the hooks. Even the lay-by, the descending slope and the numerous holes in the road.

The row of houses ended and a range of hills appeared. A bird glided across the blue sky. And down in the depths, the smell of the sea permeated everything.

Thickets of cedar trees on the right and a few yellow tents. The car stopped and let out two people with permits. The two men waved to the driver and one of them addressed him and said, 'Hope to see you again soon, dear volunteer!'

The car moved on, together with the cedar grove.

This tree is rich with leaves. That tree is thin and

naked, needles clustering thickly at its top; it looks like the hair crowning Angela Davis's head.

'You, comrade, are a university student, aren't you?' the driver said, handing him a cigarette.

He took the cigarette and lit it with difficulty, 'True, I was at the Faculty of Engineering, but I didn't like it. So I transferred to Medicine, but didn't finish the preparatory year. After that, I transferred to Literature, and now I've dropped out of that subject and have decided to join up as a volunteer.'

The driver smiled and laughed, 'Be careful then not to transfer from one organization to the other, the way you did with university faculties.'

Through the window on which dust had built up, the sky was still blue. So the volunteer, also laughing, added, 'I dream of spending an African summer in Angola next year.'

The driver slowed down and then stopped, 'You get off here, my friend, and over there at the barrier they'll lead you to the battalion headquarters.'

The volunteer held out his hand. The driver scratched his beard, offered his other hand and took leave, 'Best of luck. Hope to see you always.'

The volunteer opened the door and jumped out. The driver waved and drove off quickly.

The volunteer stamped his feet, hung his small bag over his shoulder and started walking down the road towards the thicket. He presented his papers. One of the guards accompanied him along the narrow path. He stopped at a small tent in front of which sat a young man in military uniform. He presented his papers. The young man said to him, 'We'll send a companion to guide you to the position of the group you'll be joining. You can come back in a few days to complete some formalities.'

'The position,' the companion pointed out, 'is over there by those rocks.'

The volunteer was out of breath, feeling thirsty, and his feet were swollen. His face looked haggard and worn out.

'Can I sit down for a while?'

'We can't,' said his young companion. 'There's an important military operation tonight and we ought to arrive at the position before the shooting is stepped up.'

He walked silently and so did his companion, who was more energetic. Somewhere a shell landed. It echoed deep down in the valley. Another bomb went off.

'They're bombing Arnun Citadel,' the companion said.

'Which citadel?'

'Arnun Citadel,' the young man answered. 'It's one of the citadels Salah al-Din [Saladin] built during his wars with the Crusaders. It was a supply base for his armies which marched on Palestine from this region.'

On a nearby branch, a *shinar* bird stood unstartled by the noise of the bombing. It seemed to have become used to it.

'The citadel,' the young man pointed, 'lies over there, by the highest peak visible.'

The open country, with its array of bushes, spread endlessly and the intense odour of the soil infused everything. Far away a tent was visible behind the rocks.

'We've arrived,' his companion said. 'There they are, the members of the group, looking at us.'

They were talking about the enforcement of the Cairo Agreement and about the clashes breaking out near Sabra Camp.

Abu Siraj, who had been injured in the battle of Kafr Shuba, his elbows crushed by bullet fragments, and who had gone to Hungary to have platinum joints put in, announced that what was happening was related to the visit of the American envoy.

And Ali al-Badawi, the Jordanian who wears a sheepskin over his clothes, and who specializes in mortars, said, 'What's the use of protecting al-Tiba and Rab al-Thalatheen if Sabra Camp falls?'

And Abu Arwy, who would like a sudden death, who would not like to become a deformed war victim, and who remembers his three children and his wife at Yarmuk Camp and is sad because he cannot visit them, said, 'All the roads are closed.'

And Yusif, the boy who holds an RPJ* and is a master at working the wireless, was on another wavelength altogether, and said that at the financial department they refused to give him a loan because the leadership had issued an order forbidding loans.

The volunteer sat among them. They offered him tea and, without ceremony, introduced themselves.

Here things seem legible, the volunteer thought to himself. He gazed at the open country stretching out endlessly. The open country is a poem engraved in his features, in his eyes, in his fingertips and in the movements of his hands. Here, the gentle meets with the explosive; poetry, with blood. No cafeteria, no university, no girls wearing blue jeans, no circles of debate, of esoteric discussions, of gossip or of political proselytizing.

He drank their dark, black tea and ate sardines, jam and corned beef for breakfast. At noon, he would help them prepare lunch as if he had been with them for years.

On the second day, he knew that this one was Ali al-Dhayyab al-Badawi, who loves rocks and rough roads and climbs them the way goats do. He knew that this one was Abu Siraj, who fires the *grinov* despite his elbow-joints being made of platinum, that the third one was Yusif, who bathed in cold water every day and who let his long hair cover his neck, and that the fourth one was Abu Arwy who had not seen his wife or children at the camp for over a year because he did not have a travel document and because the borders were still closed.

They would talk, take turns on guard duty, argue a little

*a Russian made gun

and dream of a holiday in Beirut or of swimming at the beach in Tyre or playing cards in the cafés of Sabra.

They have small, legitimate dreams, these young men who take to the wilderness; nobody hears of them except when they are martyred, the volunteer thought.

Yusif asked him, 'Are you going to stay with us long, my friend? It has happened before that volunteers have joined us for a month or two, but after that they have gone back to their universities.'

The volunteer gazed at Yusif's baby face. Remembering Yusif's talk in the morning about the karate film he had once seen at the Salwa Cinema, he thought that Yusif's face looked like Bruce Lee's.

He smiled and said, 'Perhaps I will stay for a long time.'

Yusif pursued, 'Did you study abroad?'

'Yes,' said the volunteer, adding, 'in Italy.'

'Is it possible for *fedaiyin* to visit Italy?'

'If the police at the airport find out that you're a *fedai*, they detain and search you, then send you on the first plane back. If you reached Rome, though, you'd find that our leftist friends would receive, indeed protect, you.'

'How much does it cost to visit Rome?'

'Do you long, young man, to travel, to explore, to acquire new things? Your dreams are perfectly legitimate. Dream on in this wide open country, its big heart is limitless.'

Abu Arwy then interrupted, 'He wants to visit Rome and we can't even visit the camp! Which one of you young men carries an ID?'

'My rifle is my ID,' Abu Siraj said jokingly.

'Why do others have passports,' Ali al-Dhayyab wondered, 'and can cross Arab borders without being stopped, while we're barred and get arrested and thrown into dungeons.'

'You're an extremist,' Abu Siraj answered him.

Meanwhile, the sound of the *doshka** rose in the

---

*a mid-range canon

distance from the snow-covered hilltop. Yusif, beside himself with joy, jumped up in the air, 'It's Said; he's opened *doshka* fire on them and taken them by surprise.'

The volunteer was quiet. The *doshka* continued to fill the open country wih its grave, roaring sound.

'Said . . . Who is Said?'

'We forgot to tell you about him. Said Abu Jaber is the commander of the *doshka* position over there.'

There, on that peak, amidst the snow, Said Abu Jaber had set up a *doshka*. On the peak that looked like a dead volcano's mouth, the snow continued to fall, killing the warmth within its depths, just like a dentist kills the nerves of the gum. He had been digging with difficulty, cutting paths through the firm snow forest for the past two months. 'Now,' said Abu Siraj, 'after these exhausting weeks, Said and his group are in control of the hill; they've broken its back. Things seem to have laid themselves open to him, yielding and coming under his control.'

From that day, Said became present in their conversations. The *doshka* did not cease operating. They spoke about him every evening.

'Said hasn't had a wink of sleep for three days.'

'Their bombs can't reach, let alone touch him.'

'Said needs blankets and woollen vests.'

The volunteer tried to envisage Said. He imagined him to be like Taras Bulba, wearing a thick belt around his waist, capable of carrying several mortars at a time on his chest, though around his head there would be a halo like that of the saints.

'Doesn't our friend, the snowman, ever come down from that peak?' the volunteer asked.

'He comes down once a month,' Ali al-Badawi answered. 'He takes a short break, but doesn't allow his assistants to come down unless to get provisions and ammunition.'

It might have been Yusif who then said in a near whisper, 'And he loves a girl called Norma.'

Norma.

Of her, they said, She is tall and slim. Her breasts aren't firm nor is her backside round. Her face and neck are freckled, but she has a pair of blue eyes. And they say that Norma is a fruit-juice seller. She owns a tin hut on the main road between Tyre and Sidon. She squeezes oranges and washes glasses, suffers from dizziness and chapped palms, and has a pale face. But when she is in good health, she glows and her eyes sparkle. Without wearing any kohl or adorning herself with jewellery, she becomes a girl fit to be loved or escorted by her lover to a ball.

According to Abu Siraj, who heard it from the administrative officer of the battalion, Said and Norma have a very close relationship. He had stopped his car once in front of her hut and asked her for a glass of fruit juice. The second time, he spoke to her gently. The third time, she became friendly, so he looked at her affectionately. Another version of the story, which Ali al-Badawi tells, has it that Said Abu Jaber has known Norma since before the war, when she had been working at the Ghandour factory. They met during the labour strike. He had been driving his military car down the main road as she was trying to stop one of the numerous cars passing through. When she waved him down, he stopped. She told him that one of the people she worked with had been injured during the suppression of the strike. So he gave her a lift to a nearby clinic. Al-Badawi adds that when Said Abu Jaber stopped while driving down the Tyre–Sidon Road past her hut after the fighting had ended, he was surprised to find her there. He ordered a glass of fruit juice. While he was drinking, she remembered who he was and so gave him his money back. She insisted and he insisted in his refusal. Finally he accepted the money on condition that she take it the next time. The second time he told her his news and she told him hers. She might have told him that she had become a Dikwana Lane refugee, that her old mother lived in the refugees' huts at Ouzai and that she now works as a juice seller and suffers from anaemia and the molestation of truck drivers. The third time, he looked at her affectionately and she looked at him with familiarity. He said nothing to her; she in turn said nothing to him. But after that, Said Abu Jaber would visit her during his monthly vacation to drink a glass of juice. He would tell her about the sting of the snow and the frost which never ends and she would tell him about her small worries or those that were insurmountable.

'The open country, valleys and plains, grass, flowers, birds, nests, space, evening, fog. The open country has its own dictionary, vocabulary and alphabet. Arnun Citadel is high, towering. Through the fog, it appears redolent of history and secrets. Is it true that Salah al-din built it? And did his men pass through these lands? During the nights when the shooting stops, I can almost hear the neighing of their horses. And when the savage winds blow, I smell the memories which they planted in these regions just as they used to plant flowers in the hair of their mistresses and words in the rhythms of their poems.'

Off duty, the volunteer begins to clean his weapon. Then he puts a bullet in the muzzle and fires it in the air. A flock of birds flies off; a turtle comes out carrying its shell on its back, moving slowly. The sun disappears suddenly behind a veil of clouds. The journey of the fog begins. The whole valley is afloat with moving vapour. The drizzle falls. The fortress hides its head and its body settles in, and the shell is left naked. The volunteer opens a can of sardines and eats hastily. He throws away the empty can.

Yusif, who dreams of being on a plane and seeing Rome, says, 'Why are they afraid of us at airports, volunteer?'

'Because we hijack planes.'

'Are you against hijacking planes?'

'Yes, I am.'

'Why?'

'Because I'm against terrorism and operations outside our land.'

'What does it mean, to be against terrorism and outside operations?'

The volunteer began to explain, using his fingers and hands, getting worked up, his features changing . . .

By the cedar trees, Abu Awry was collecting dry firewood. Ali al-Dhayyab slung his rifle over his shoulder and walked to the well two kilometres away to wash. Suddenly the volunteer stopped talking.

Yusif looked at the road in surprise, and said, 'Here's Said; he's come at last! Said, Said Abu Jaber!'

He was walking wrapped in sheepskin, leaning on a stick. His thick beard made him look like a forest ranger living in the wilderness.

He bears strong muscles on his arms and chest. He seems at first sight like a man as strong as a thousand horses.

Abu Siraj came over. From afar Ali al-Dhayyab fired two shots in the air in greeting. He saluted them warmly.

In the evening, glasses of tea went round. They conversed and exchanged the latest news and stories about the snow and the frost. Glasses of tea went round once more. Outside, the snow began falling. He took out his packet of cigarettes and offered one to each. Then he lit one . . . and then another . . . and then a third. So Abu Siraj said, 'Said, you smoke non-stop. If we laid all the cigarettes you've smoked in your life end to end, they'd go all the way around the Mediterranean.'

When it was time for his turn to guard, the volunteer got up and excused himself, picked up his rifle and left. The snow stopped falling. Having fallen in a thin layer, the snow began to melt, forming small waterfalls which flowed down to the valley. He heard a scrabbling sound in the grass. He approached, and picked up a handful of wet thorns. Two panic-stricken eyes and a terrified body appeared. It was a white rabbit, like a piece of cotton. He moved closer. Both ears straightened. Nose trembled. He bent over and carried the rabbit by its ears. It resisted weakly and then calmed down. He walked back. The bombs were falling far away, the fog was thickening and the extreme cold penetrated through to the bones.

He entered the tent. Abu Siraj was setting light to a pile of firewood. He lifted the rabbit by its ears in front of them and said, 'I found him in the middle of the thorns, nearly dead from the frost and the cold.'

Said stretched out his hand and took the wild rabbit and put it in front of him near the burning firewood. The rabbit remained still, its belly moving up and down slowly, breathing the way children do. It was still except for its two violet eyes animated by an intense expression of pain.

The volunteer went out. Evening was approaching. In the distance, a light signal shone. It sank down gradually as it if were a lantern falling from the sky. The trees remained quiet and the branches still. The frogs stopped croaking.

Finally, Said Abu Jaber came out with his sheepskin, thick beard, muscles and stick and said, 'Warmth, my friend, is creeping into your rabbit's bones. Soon, he will recover.' He smiled, adding, 'I'm off to Sidon. Do you need anything?'

'In this weather?' the astonished volunteer asked.

He smiled again and said, 'Don't worry, my friend. My car is powerful and I'm still in good health. So farewell!'

Clouds of breath emerged from his mouth and nostrils. He walked off confidently as if he was four men in one. He climbed into his car, which he had parked at the end of the road and drove off.

'Said has gone to see Norma.'

'But the fog is thick and the road is full of danger.'

'If he doesn't see Norma, all the war gods will not be able to make him hold out on that snow mountain.'

'What is it that he likes about that weak, pale girl, who has a flat bosom and ankles like a stork's?'

'Looks don't count; she is very beautiful inside. Deep inside, she is full of the fragrance of humanity.'

'Said is getting closer as the camp recedes into the distance.'

'Said travels to his love; he keeps on travelling.'

'And the rabbit near the firewood has begun either waking up or falling asleep.'

'More light signals are shining. They fear a sudden attack by our forces in the other sector.'

Ali al-Dhayyab returned after a long absence. He washed himself with cold water and washed his underwear. In spite of his pride, he started shivering again and his teeth began to knock against each other. So he charged into the tent, and stretched out his arm to the fire's glow. The rabbit was yielding to the warmth and seemed like a little pet cat.

Glasses of hot tea went round. Yusif began to work on the wireless. Now, the volunteer thought to himself, now Said is arriving at the tin hut. Norma comes out to receive him. Norma, with the skinny body, the freckled face and blue eyes. His big palm receives her tiny, rough palm, smelling of orange peel. Her eyes arouse in him the soil's yearning for the rain and the sap's union with the roots.

The warmth flowed through Ali al-Dhayyab's fingers and arms. Abu Siraj and Abu Awry began to get ready to sleep. Ali al-Dhayyab kept patting the rabbit on its back and stroking its shiny white fur with his palm. The volunteer went back to talking to himself. The world of these men is full of the fragrance of humanity. Deep inside, they are rich in kindness and experience. When I have a proper experience, I will ride the back of snow-covered mountains and dream like the wild man of the open country, whose power is said to be as great as eighty horses. He remembered the driver who brought him from Nabatia military headquarters to the post and said to himself, if I meet him, he'll say, 'In the beginning everything seems unusual, but as the days pass, you lose this feeling of astonishment; isn't that so, volunteer?' 'Volunteer' will become my code name. Perhaps no one will ask about my real name and the name of my village will not be known. But if I were injured in battle, three of them would give their lives to save me.

Abu Siraj was in a deep slumber and Abu Arwy was sleeping silently, breathing quietly. Perhaps he is dreaming of his three children at the refugee camp and his face will light up with joy. The murmur of the water outside continued to lend dignity to this silence. Yusif turned off the wireless and began to get ready to sleep.

It was a sunny morning. The layer of snow melted. The water continued to dwindle away until it had seeped completely into the ground. Life suddenly coursed through the white rabbit. It moved about the tent. The volunteer's face lit up with joy and he carried the rabbit about, as it breathed out warmth. He carried it in his arms and woke up the comrades, who formed a circle around him, watching the rabbit and playing with it. After that, they went to prepare breakfast. The wireless began working again. Birds filled the sky. Nobody bothered about the reconnaissance planes flying high. The rabbit remained quiet in the hands of the volunteer, staring with a pair of violet eyes without trembling.

Said came back the following afternoon. Once again, he arrived with his sheepskin, his thick beard and his stick. He was wearing a woollen cap on his head. He arrived smiling and carrying in his hands a box of sweets which he gave to Yusif, and said, 'For you and the friends.'

'So, it was a successful visit,' Ali al-Dhayyab said.

Said Abu Jaber laughed and all at once burst out, saying, 'Next time, she'll come with me and volunteer. She too will become a volunteer.'

He looked at the volunteer, who smiled. He imagined the skinny woman who has blue eyes and sells juice. He tried to find her a task amongst them but couldn't imagine her as anything but a wireless operator.

Said became aware of the rabbit in the volunteer's arms and said, 'How's your rabbit, volunteer?'

'He has recovered and is well now.'

The man with the strong muscles, said to be as powerful as eighty horses, seemed joyful and carefree. He appeared so buoyant, delicate, sensitive, transparent. The glasses of tea went round, and Said apologized, saying, 'I have to get back to my position out there.'

And before they could interrupt him, he offered them cigarettes and lit one himself. 'I can't be late, comrades,' he said holding out his hand. 'Farewell.'

And before turning around, he looked at the rabbit in the volunteer's arms and said, 'Don't slaughter the rabbit, dear friend.'

The volunteer looked at the rabbit, which seemed to be on the alert, and at its eyes with their sweet sparkle.

'Do we set it free?' Ali al-Dhayyab said.

Said Abu Jaber nodded.

The volunteer bent down and put the rabbit on the ground. The rabbit gazed out at the open country for a few moments and then jumped. It swooped away, hopping high and far in the grass and then disappeared between the cedar trees. Said smiled, and then smiled, and then smiled yet again, and then waved to them. He turned around, got into his military car and drove off up the rough road.

Over there, up there, way up there, the peak was wrapped in a mantle of snow.

And over the peak of the hill, a big white cloud darted past.

'A cloud, white like the wild rabbits,' the volunteer said.

And Yusif said, 'It travels and never stops travelling.'

'And it will glide across the sky above the camp,' Abu Awry said.

And Abu Siraj said, 'A cloud, silvery and white, like a wedding dress for a tall, thin woman with a pair of blue eyes and a face full of freckles.'

Translated by Magda Amin and Nur Elmessiri

Breaking the Silence

Ghareeb Asqalani

News Item

There was a rumour going round that the belly of one of the wives in the camp had swollen despite her husband's absence. This rumour took over people's thoughts, and the merchants in the prosperous wholesale markets panicked. The news spread quickly, insinuating itself into every house.

The wife was a pretty girl, with an air of ripe fertility, and the husband was not like the other men . . . or so the people of the camp said.

A Report by a Man from the Masses,
Independent of the Sultan

I know that the girl Salma is always smiling. She is one of the beauties of the camp. She was the daughter of the silent sheikh and was engaged to the tall young man who was known throughout the camp as 'the knight'. I also know that the knight was fond of throwing oranges at flocks of crows on moonlit nights.

I can testify that on the night of his wedding the knight neglected his bride. It was said that he was busy throwing oranges as usual. It was also said that the crows, recognizing him, spread out and gave chase. This is why he vanished, failing to return to his bride at nightfall as is customary, so that nobody knew for certain whether he had embraced her by dawn. What is certain, however, is that till today the young bride's smile has not deserted her.

Days have passed since the event of the wedding night, and no one has seen the tall knight.

These are my comments.

1

Her belly grew rounder, she became more radiant, her body, elated, swayed and she walked about, head held high, looking lovingly at people. The women looked on the thing dazzled. One of them said, 'Is it pregnancy?'

Another, spitting to drive the devil from her bosom, retorted, 'I wouldn't like to say, God only knows.'

And so the women, quite unlike themselves, held their tongues, for the coming days would reveal all.

2

Her belly rose and her eyes lit up like wedding lanterns. She told the good news to the old sheikh sitting in his corner, observing the life of the world. He wept, this time for joy, while she stroked her belly. She loosened the belt around her waist fearing it might be tight. She went about singing to the children in the camp's alleyways and greeting the women. One said knowingly, 'This is pregnancy.'

Another replied, 'That cannot be concealed from anyone.'

And quite unlike themselves the women, fearing God, held their tongues. The matter continued to perplex them . . .

How had it happened? Could it have happened? And when?

And silence prevailed.

3

The silence was rent by whispers about the knight. Some years ago the crows had chased him after the lavish wedding feast . . . then it was said he was dead though the body never came to light . . . they said the crows had torn him apart, but this piece of news was never verified.

Some friends questioned the old skeikh as he sat in his corner observing the world. He stared in silence at a distant circle of light.

It was rumoured that the knight had headed east, towards his friends. They said that because the corners of the earth had become too tight, he left.

The sheikh smiled, no one knew what the sheikh's smile meant.

4

'Fertility is beginning to flow in her breasts,' the old midwife said, adding, 'I've never seen a girl produce milk so soon before her time.'

The women were affronted.

'Can this make sense?'

The old woman held her peace. The women fell silent and took to keeping an eye on the girl. They grew more perplexed than ever for the milk of her breasts had indeed come before its time. Cautiously, they emerged from their silence.

5

'I've seen the knight!' called a boy joyfully.

The woman looked round, clapped her hand over the boy's mouth and dragged him into the house. Expecting a calamity, she yelled, 'Liar! Don't ever say such a thing again!'

The boy was startled; disappointed. Why was his mother angry? Had he not heard her and the other women say that the knight had . . . and had . . . and had . . . He shouted in defiance, 'I swear I saw him!' He continued emphatically, 'Ask the bride.'

'I'll tell your father, then you'll be sorry you lied.'

'Tell him then and I'll tell him how I saw the knight.'

What persistence . . . the child . . . could it be . . . him so defiant, so sure of himself . . . his mother drew him close and whispered, 'How did you see him?'

The boy told his story. And the next day another boy spoke up, then a third, until all the boys in the alley were repeating the first boy's tale. And the old midwife laughed as she had never laughed before, embracing the boys who had confirmed that the milk of the bride had indeed come before its time.

6

The boy said, as the other boys said, 'In the evening I was looking at Salma's belly. She smiled at me and began to stroke my hair, singing and kissing me. We continued playing till dawn. Salma unbraided her hair, shook it lose, and asked me, "What do you see?"

'I could see nothing except her golden bundle of hair. She caressed me and laid my head on her lap. She squeezed some of her breast milk into my eyes and asked what I saw. I saw the knight approaching . . . a wedding, ululations and song. He kept coming towards us until he embraced us and laid his head down on Salma's lap next to me. And so we dozed until the songs were complete, and then we woke.'

The woman asked, 'And how did you know that the songs were complete?'

'I don't know – the songs were complete and we awoke.'

'Then what happened?'

'Nothing. Salma and I returned and the knight went away.'

'And where were you and Salma?'

The child fell silent and the woman was filled with wonder. The child knows other things . . . his eyes are insistent. But what does he know? Can he be believed? The thing that continued to perplex the women was that the boys carried on repeating the same story and the midwife kept vouching for their honesty. The women kept silence over the children's stories and did not tell the men.

7

Labour drew near.

The old woman was filled with energy and renewed vigour.

The old sheikh came out of his corner where he sat watching life in the heart of the camp, gazing at the youngsters, yearning . . . when will it come and fill the alley with cries and with chatter?

'The young woman's womb has ripened,' said the dazzled midwife.

The women broke their silence.

Labour, labour. Tongues wagged. The news reached the ears of the men, and at first they were cautious and then reacted with joy. The news spread. It became the only topic of conversation from morning till night. The men spread the news without fear.

The news enveloped the alley, for the guilt was a shared guilt. To cover up a burgeoning womb, ripening, would be shameful, so no matter. They talked at length. When will it come? Desire for the child was increasing . . . becoming a wave . . . a yearning . . . for the knight would emerge from a burgeoning womb.

Advice to stay near the girl was heaped down on the women. Nor did the men forget to prepare gifts. Knitting needles clicked away producing clothes and blankets, outdoing themselves in making the most beautiful gown for the expected child.

8

The men came home from work unusually early. Drawing near the camp their worries and exhaustion dropped away. The girl sat on the floor in the room surrounded by the women. She parted her thighs to widen the birth passage. She laughed in the women's faces. She gasped. Tears of happiness coursed down her cheeks. The waters burst forth, announcing the beginning of arrival.

The man said, 'Today I threw an orange pip at the paper factory; it burned down and the crows were suffocated.'

The girl gave birth.

The old midwife delivered the news. 'The child is like his father.'

Silence prevailed as the ululations died down, for the sultan's men had spread out, investigating the matter of the orange and the suffocating of the crows. But the old sheikh refused to return to his corner before telling the youngsters of the alleys the good news.

A Report by a Man who Prays to the Sultan
This news is without doubt a rumour.

No one can escape the punishment of the crows.

The knight is a legend in the minds of the illiterate.

The wife is pregnant by a casual visitor and the expected child a bastard.

People must not believe the rumour. Stability and more stability must be maintained for the merchants. Good luck to them with soaring prices! I recommend that my master the sultan officially deny the rumour.

Excerpt from an UNRWA Report
We were informed by one of the camp schools that a child enrolled in first primary had refused to disclose his father's name as a precaution against the sultan's men. After some insistence the child registered his father's name as 'the knight'. We have no choice but to inform you

that we registered him under his mother's name 'Salma – daughter of the silent sheikh'.

Appendix
A man from the masses, independent of the sultan, related that the child reproached his grandfather. Then he tore up his ration card and threw it on to the rubbish dump. The grandfather did not become angry; rather, he emerged from his silence for ever and went about overseeing the alleyways of the camp.

Translated by Karaz Mona Hamdy and Nur Elmessiri

Brief Biographies of the Writers

Rashad Abu Shawer (b. 1942)
Writer and activist. He was born in the village of Zikrin,
Hebron, but was forced to leave for Jordan in the after-
math of the 1948 war. He has been active in the
Palestinian resistance movement since the late 1960s.
Many of his short stories have been translated into
English, French, German, Farsi, Russian, etc. His works
include:
  Trees Never Grow on Books (short stories, 1975)
  Lovers (novel, 1977)
  Pizza in Memory of Mariam (short stories, 1981)

Rasmi Abu Ali (b. 1937)
Poet, novelist and journalist. He was born near Jerusalem,
and settled in Jordan after 1948. He studied in Cairo
where he stayed on and contributed to the Arab literary
press. His works incude:
  A Cat with Clipped Whiskers Called Rayyis (short
    stories, 1980)
  It Does Not Resemble this River (poetry, 1984)
  The Road to Bethlehem (novel, 1985)

Salih Abu Isbaa (b. 1947)
Writer, journalist and university lecturer. He was born in
the village of Salama, Jaffa. He received a PhD in Arabic
Literature in 1977 and a PhD in Mass Communications

in 1982. His works include:
  Naked on the River Bank (short stories, 1972)
  Trial of a Tall Man (short stories, 1974)
  The Water Princess (short stories, 1977)
  Stand Up . . . Laugh (short stories, 1991)

Ghareeb Asqalani (b. 1948)
The pen name of Ibrahim al-Zont, writer and teacher of
Arabic. He was born in the town of al-Majdal, Gaza Strip.
He currently lives and works in Gaza. His works include:
  Breaking the Silence (short stories, 1979)
  The Collar (novel, 1979)

Samira Azzam (1927–1967)
Writer, broadcaster and translator. She was born in Acre,
and in 1948 fled with her family first to Beirut and then to
Baghdad, where she worked as a teacher for two years. She
returned to Beirut, became involved in literary activities
and participated in several radio programmes in Cyprus
and Baghdad. Her works include:
  Little Things (short stories, 1954)
  The Big Shadow (short stories, 1956)
  The Feast from the Western Window (short stories,
    posthumously published in 1971)

Liana Badr (b. 1950)
Writer, journalist and activist. She was born in Jerusalem,
and after the 1967 war she left for Amman, then moved to
Beirut and Tunis before finally returning to Ramallah.
She was a volunteer in welfare programmes at Palestinian
refugee camps in Jordan and Lebanon from 1969 to 1976.
Her works include:
  A Compass for the Sunflower (novel, 1979)
  A Balcony Over the Fakahany Quarter (short stories,
    1983)
  Tales of Love and Pursuit (short stories, 1983)
  I Want the Daylight (short stories, 1985)
  The Eye of the Mirror (novel, 1991)

Riyad Baidas (b. 1960)
Writer and journalist. He was born in the village of Shafa
'Amr, Haifa and still lives there. His works include:
   Hunger and the Mountain (short stories, 1980)
   The Wind (short stories, 1987)
   A Faint Sound (short stories, 1990)

Zaki Darwish (b. 1944)
Writer and translator. He was born in the village of al-
Birwa, Acre. After the destruction of his village by Israeli
forces in 1948, he sought refuge for a short time in
Lebanon, later returning to Acre, where he lives and
works as a secondary school principal. His works include:
   The Bridge and the Deluge (short stories, 1973)
   The Man Who Killed the World (short stories, 1978)
   Ahmed, Mahmoud and Others (novel, 1989)

Tawfiq Fayyad (b. 1939)
Writer and activist. He was born in the village of
Muqeibila, Jenin. In 1970, he was detained by Israeli
authorities for activities aiming to preserve the cultural
heritage of Palestine. In 1974, he was forcibly deported to
Egypt. He currently lives in Tunis. Among his works are:
   The Yellow Road (short stories, 1967)
   Group No. 778 (novel, 1975)
   The Fool (short stories, 1978)

Emile Habibi (1921–1996)
Novelist, journalist and activist. He was born in the
village of Shafa 'Amr, Haifa, and has taken part in political
activities since the early 1940s. He was a member of the
Communist Party in Israel, and after its split belonged to
the largely Arab section: The New Communist List –
RAKAH. He was a member of the Knesset from 1953 till
1972. He was awarded the State of Israel Prize for
Literature in 1992. His works include:
   The Hexad of the Six Days (short stories, 1969)

The Strange Circumstances Around the Disappearance
    of Said Abi al-Nahs, the Pessoptimist (novel, 1974)
Soraya, the Ghoul's Daughter (novel, 1991)

Hassan Hemeid (b. 1955)

Writer and journalist. He was born in the village of al-Baqqarah, Safed, and sought refuge in Damascus where he still lives. He has been a regular contributor to the Arabic press. His works include:

Twelve Towers for Borj al-Brajna (short stories, 1983)
Roar of the Dead (short stories, 1987)
The Pigeons Flew (short stories, 1988)
Departure from al-Baqqarah (novel, 1988)

Ghassan Kanafani (1936–1972)

Writer, critic, activist and a leading member of the resistance organization, the Popular Front for the Liberation of Palestine – PFLP. He was born in Acre, and after the 1948 war he was forced to leave his native land and seek refuge in Damascus, Kuwait and Beirut. He contributed extensively to the Arab press during the 1950s and 1960s, and in 1969 became editor-in-chief of *al-Hadaf* (*Target*), the organ of the PFLP. On 8 July 1972, he was assassinated by Mossad agents in Beirut, while at the peak of his creative powers. His works include:

Men in the Sun (novel, 1963)
What Remains to You (novel, 1966)
Om Saad (novel, 1969)
Returning to Haifa (novel, 1970)
Death of Bed No. 12 (short stories, 1961)
Land of Sad Oranges (short stories, 1963)
Of Men and Guns (short stories, 1968)
Resistance Literature in Palestine (criticism, 1966)
On Zionist Literature (criticism, 1967)

Mohamed Naffaa (b. 1940)

Writer and politician. He was born in the village of Beit

Jann, Acre, and still resides there. Since 1970, he has been a member of the Israeli opposition party: The New Communist List – RAKAH. Many of his writings have been translated into English, French, Hebrew, Russian and Spanish. His works include:

The North Wind (short stories, 1979)
Meadow of Gazelles (novel, 1982)
Kushan (short stories, 1990)

Jamal Naji (b. 1954)

Novelist. He was born at Aqabet Jabr refugee camp, Jericho. He was forced to leave his native land twice, in 1948 and 1967. He currently lives in Amman. His works include:

The Road to Belharat (novel, 1982)
Time (novel, 1984)
Debris of the Last Storms (novel, 1988)
An Empty-Headed Man (short stories, 1989)

Ahmed Omar Shaheen (b. 1940)

Novelist, critic, and compiler of a number of encyclopaedic dictionaries. He was born in Jaffa, then settled in Gaza after 1948. He studied in Cairo where he now lives, and he contributes to the Arab press. His works include:

A House for Stoning, a House for Prayer (novel, 1989)
Situations (short stories, 1992)
Encyclopaedia of Palestinian Men of Letters in the Twentieth Century (1992)

Mahmoud al-Rimawi (b. 1948)

Writer and journalist. He was born in the town of Beit Rima, Ramallah, and has been a regular contributor to many Arabic newspapers and magazines. His works include:

Nakedness in a Night Desert (short stories, 1972)
A Planet of Apples and Salts (short stories, 1987)
A Slow Beat on a Small Drum (short stories, 1991)

Akram Shareem (b. 1942)
Writer and journalist. He was born in the town of
Qalqiliya, Tulkarm, but left for Syria in 1948 where he has
lived ever since. His works include:
> *We Are Not Dead Yet* (short stories, 1967)
> *The Prisoners Do Not Fight* (short stories, 1972)
> *Captives of the Plague* (short stories, 1988)

Mahmoud Shuqair (b. 1941)
Writer and journalist. He was born in Jersualem and was
detained many times by the Israeli authorities because of
his political and cultural activities, till in 1975 he was
deported to Amman. His works include:
> *Others' Bread* (short stories, 1975)
> *The Palestinian Boy* (short stories, 1977)
> *The Soldier and the Game* (1990)

Mohamed Ali Taha (b. 1941)
Writer and politician. He was born in the village of Mi'ar
Acre, and after the destruction of his native village during
the 1948 war, he sought refuge in a neighbouring village,
Kabul, where he currently lives. Since the late 1970s, he
has been politically active with The Democratic Front for
Peace and Equality – DFPE; a coalition of Jewish and Arab
left-wing organizations, whose members are mainly
Palestinians. His works include:
> *For the Sun to Rise* (short stories, 1964)
> *A Bridge Over the Sad River* (short stories, 1974)
> *To Be in the Coming Era* (short stories, 1989)

Mohamed Tamila (b. 1957)
Writer and teacher of Arabic at the University of Jordan,
and editor in chief of the magazine *al-Raseef*. His works
include:
> *The Disappointment* (short stories)
> *The Enthusiastic Rogues* (short stories)

Farouk Wadi (b. 1949)
Writer and journalist. He was born in the village of al-Bira,
Ramallah. After the 1967 war, he left for Egypt, then went
to Beirut and finally to Amman. His works include:
>   *Exile, My Beloved* (short stories, 1976)
>   *A Path to the Sea* (novel, 1980)
>   *Three Landmarks in the History of the Palestinian
>   Novel* (criticism, 1981)

Yehia Yakhlaf (b. 1944)
Writer, activist and Secretary-General of the Union of
Palestinian Writers and Journalists – UPWJ from 1980 till
1984. He was born in the village of Samakh, Tiberias. He
currently lives in Tunis, where he worked as a cultural
counsellor to the PLO chairman, Yasser Arafat. Among
his works are:
>   *The Filly* (short stories, 1972)
>   *Norma and the Snowman* (short stories, 1978)
>   *The Song of Life* (novel, 1985)
>   *That Rose of a Woman* (novella, 1990)

Notes on the Translators

Magda Amin teaches in the Freshman Writing Program of the American University in Cairo where she obtained her BA and MA in English and Comparative Literature. She received her PhD from Vienna University, the dissertation for which was a comparative study of Rainer Maria Rilke and Salah Abd al-Sabour.

Anthony Calderbank teaches in the Freshman Writing Program of the American University in Cairo. He studied Arabic at Manchester University from which he obtained his BA and then went onto get an MA in Applied Linguistics at Salford University. He has taught Arabic for many years.

Randa Elgeyoushi works as an English radio announcer and as a translator in Cairo. She attended school in England, where she lived for many years, and then went on to receive a BA in English Literature from Ain Shams University, Cairo.

Hala Halim works on the Culture and Profile pages of *AL-Ahram Weekly* where she writes, commissions and translates articles. She obtained her BA in English Literature from Alexandria University and went on to receive an MA in English and Comparative Literature from the American University in Cairo, the dissertation for which was a comparative study of Alexandria in the work of Lawrence Durrell, Edward al-Kharrat and Anatole France.

Karaz Mona Hamdy is a freelance translator. She received her school education in England where she lived for many years and then went on to obtain a BA in English and Comparative Literature at the American University in Cairo.

Sahar Hamouda is a lecturer in English Literature at Alexandria University where she obtained her BA, MA and PhD, the dissertation for which was on Christopher Isherwood and autobiographical fiction. She has written several articles on comparative literature which is where her current research interests lie.